THIS DIARY BELONGS TO:

Nikki J. Maxwell

PRIVATE & CONFIDENTIAL

If found, please return to ME for REWARD!

(NO SNOOPING ALLOWED!!!☹)

Have you read all these books by Rachel Renée Russell?

DORK DIARIES

Dork Diaries
Party Time
Pop Star
Skating Sensation
Dear Dork
Holiday Heartbreak
TV Star
Once Upon a Dork
Drama Queen
Puppy Love
Frenemies Forever

How to Dork Your Diary
OMG!: All About Me Diary!

THE MISADVENTURES OF MAX CRUMBLY

Locker Hero
Middle School Mayhem

Rachel Renée Russell

DORK
diaries

crush catastrophe

with Nikki Russell and Erin Russell

SIMON AND SCHUSTER

First published in Great Britain in 2017 by Simon and Schuster UK Ltd
A CBS COMPANY

First published in the USA in 2017 as Dork Diaries 12: Tales from a Not-So-Secret Crush Catastrophe
by Aladdin, an imprint of Simon & Schuster Children's Publishing Division.

Copyright © 2017 Rachel Renée Russell
Series design by Lisa Vega
The text of this book was set in Skippy Sharp

1 3 5 7 9 10 8 6 4 2

Simon & Schuster UK Ltd
1st Floor, 222 Gray's Inn Road
London WC1X 8HB

Simon & Schuster Australia, Sydney
Simon & Schuster India, New Delhi

A CIP catalogue record for this book is available from the British Library.

HB ISBN: 978-1-4711-6775-1
Export PB ISBN: 978-1-4711-6801-7
eBook ISBN: 978-1-4711-6776-8

Printed and bound by CPI Group (UK) Ltd, Croydon, CR0 4YY

MIX
Paper from
responsible sources
FSC® C020471

Simon & Schuster UK Ltd are committed to sourcing paper
that is made from wood grown in sustainable forests and support the Forest
Stewardship Council, the leading international forest certification organisation.
Our books displaying the FSC logo are printed on FSC certified paper.

www.simonandschuster.co.uk
www.simonandschuster.com.au

www.dorkdiaries.co.uk

To all of my Dork Diaries fans
with a secret crush.

You know who you are ☺!

WEDNESDAY, MAY 21—7:15 A.M.
AT HOME

SQUEEEEEE ☺!! I think I'm suffering from a severe case of CRUSH-ITIS!!

OMG! I wonder if I'm actually falling in . . .

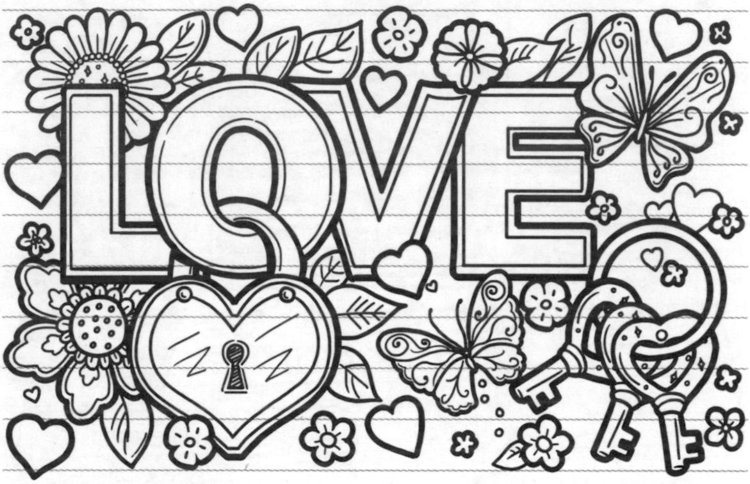
LOVE

. . . because I feel so INSANELY happy, I could VOMIT sunshine, rainbows, confetti, glitter, and those cute little Skittles candy thingies! My heart is pounding, my palms are sweaty, and the butterflies fluttering around inside my stomach are making me feel a little queasy.

Unfortunately, there is no known CURE. . . .

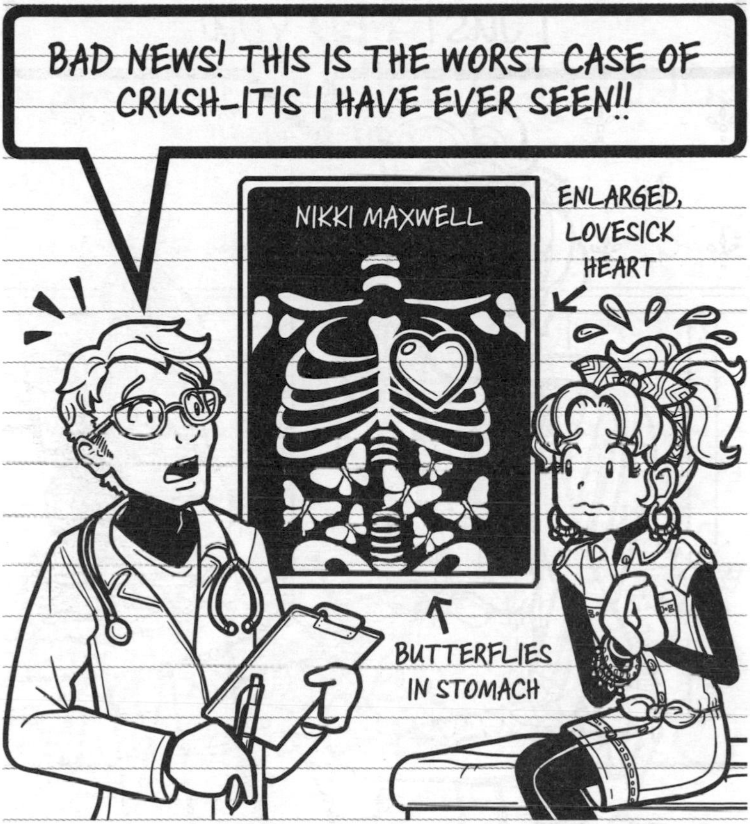
BAD NEWS! THIS IS THE WORST CASE OF CRUSH-ITIS I HAVE EVER SEEN!!
NIKKI MAXWELL
ENLARGED, LOVESICK HEART
BUTTERFLIES IN STOMACH

MY CRUSH-ITIS DIAGNOSIS

How I got this acute case of crush-itis is kind of a long and complicated story. I was just about to eat breakfast and head off to school. . . .

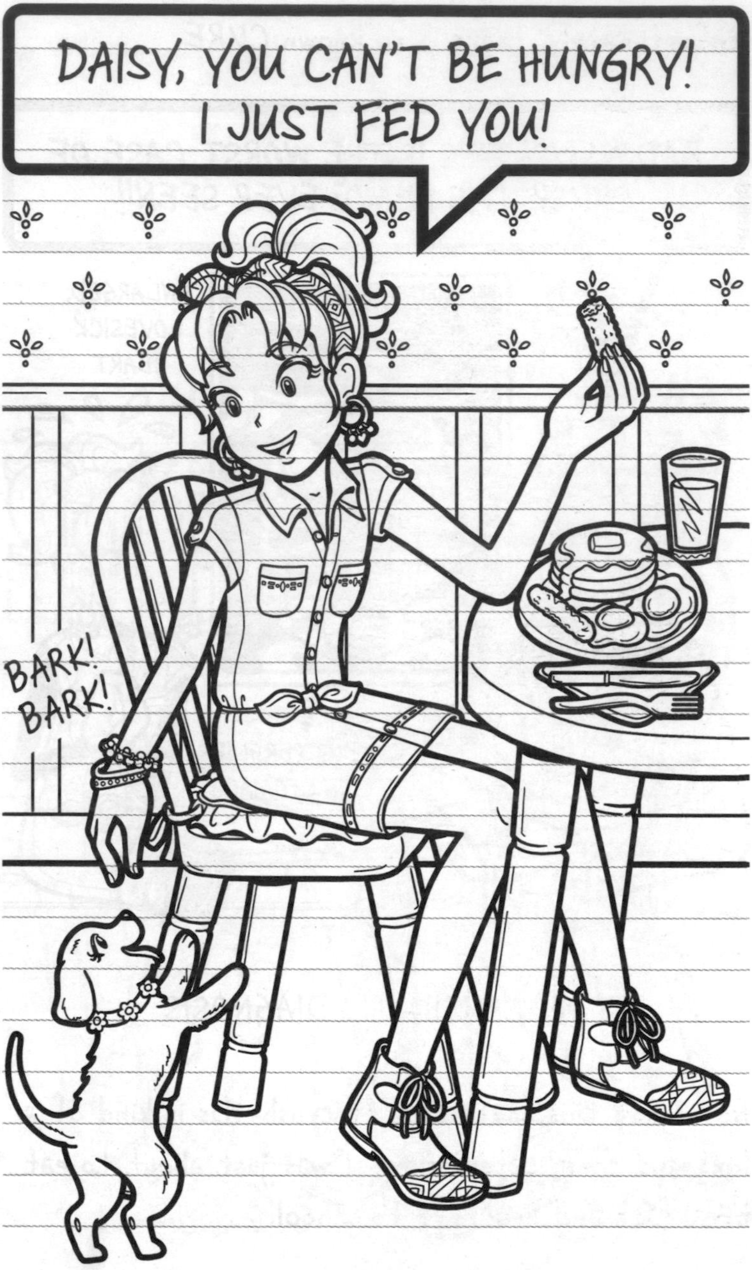
DAISY, YOU CAN'T BE HUNGRY! I JUST FED YOU!
BARK! BARK!

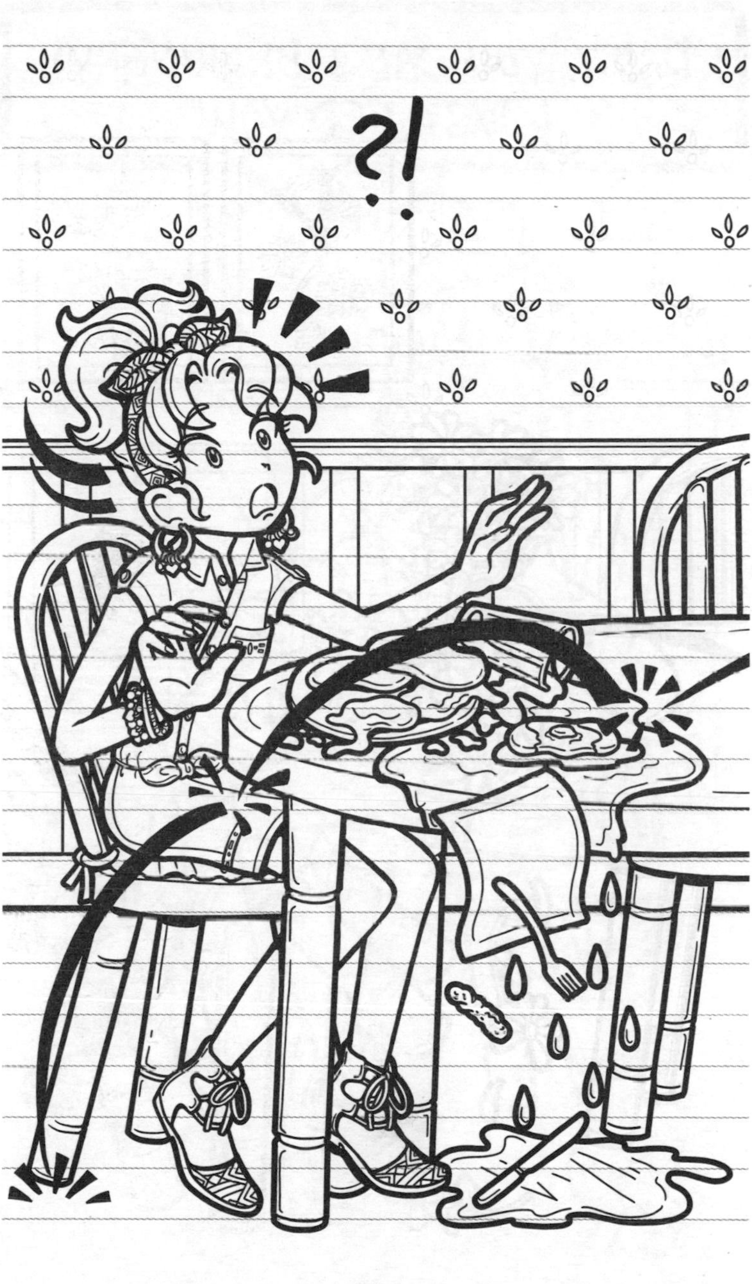
?!

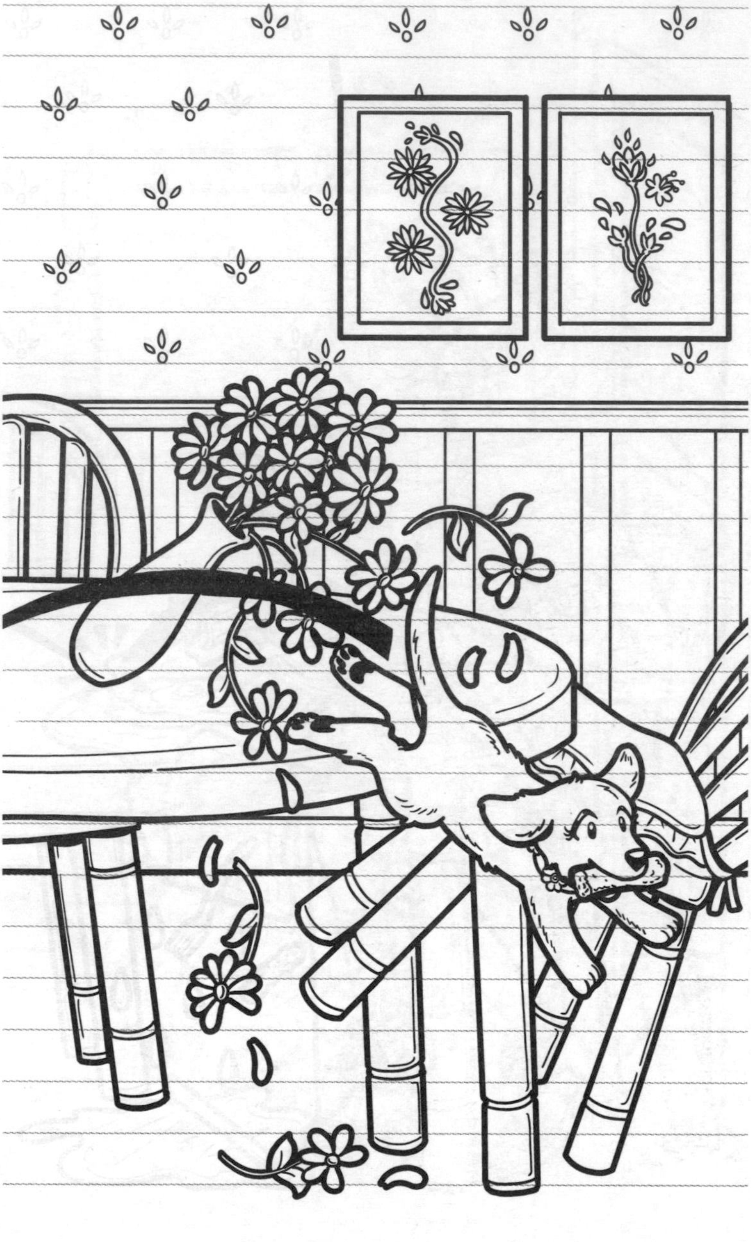

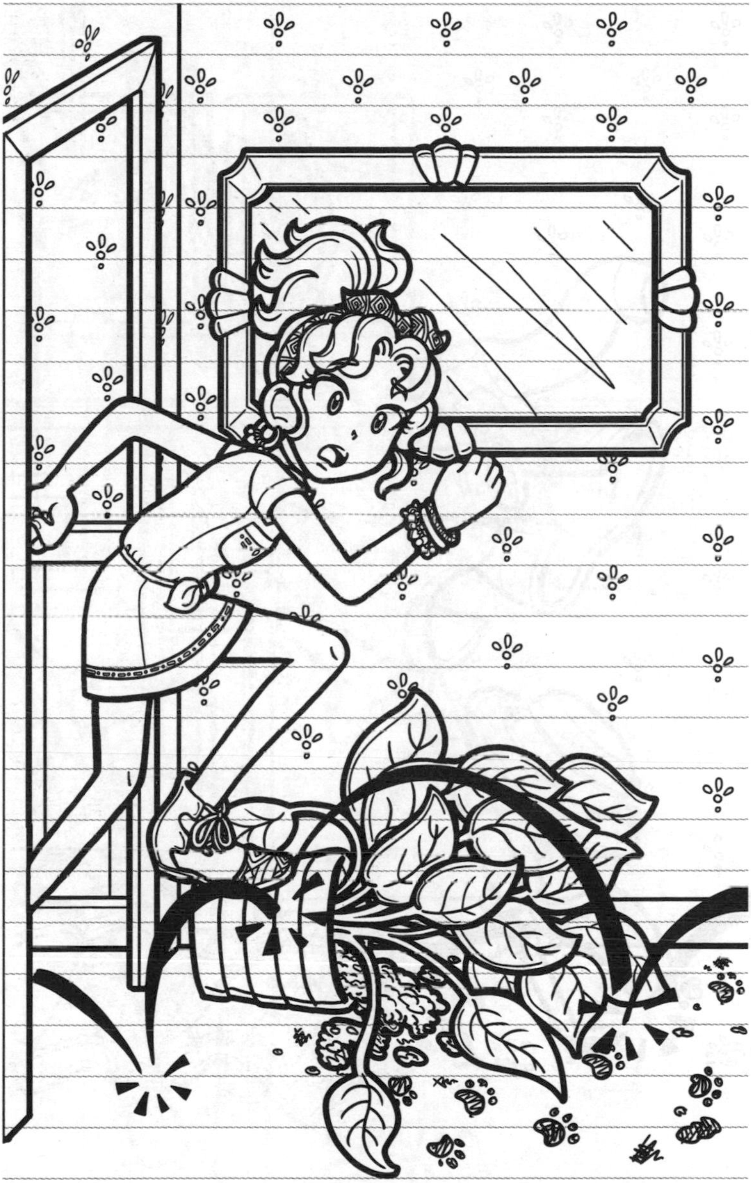

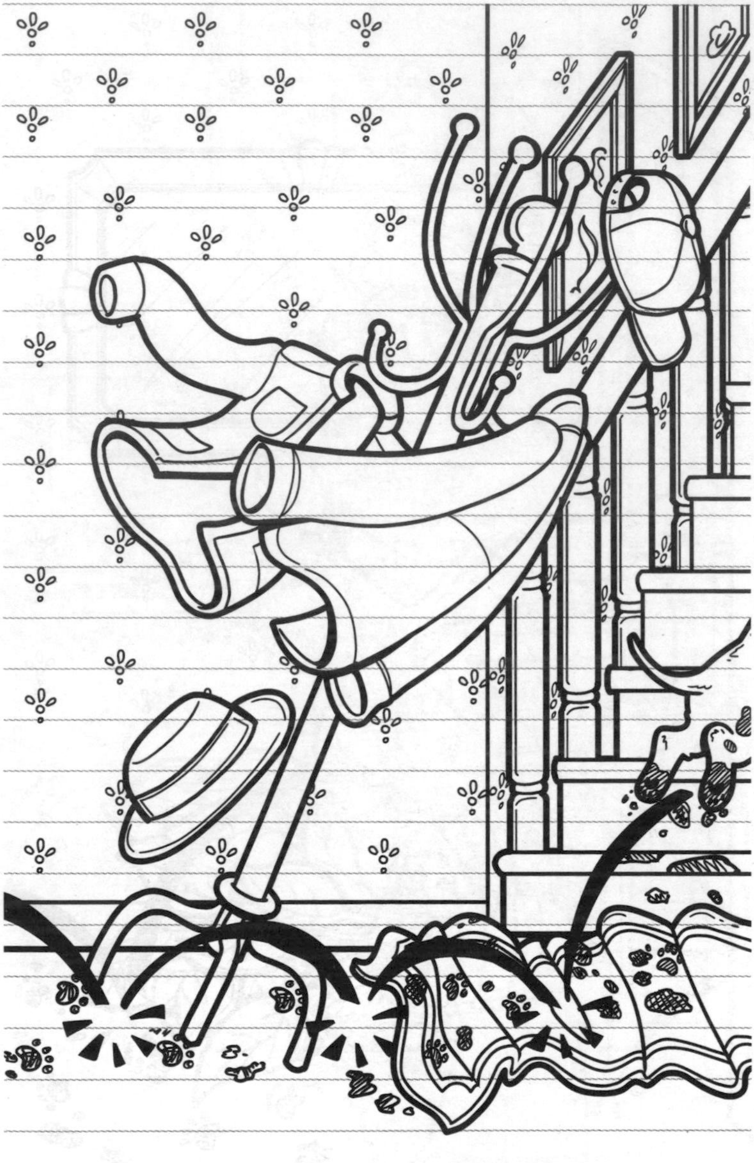

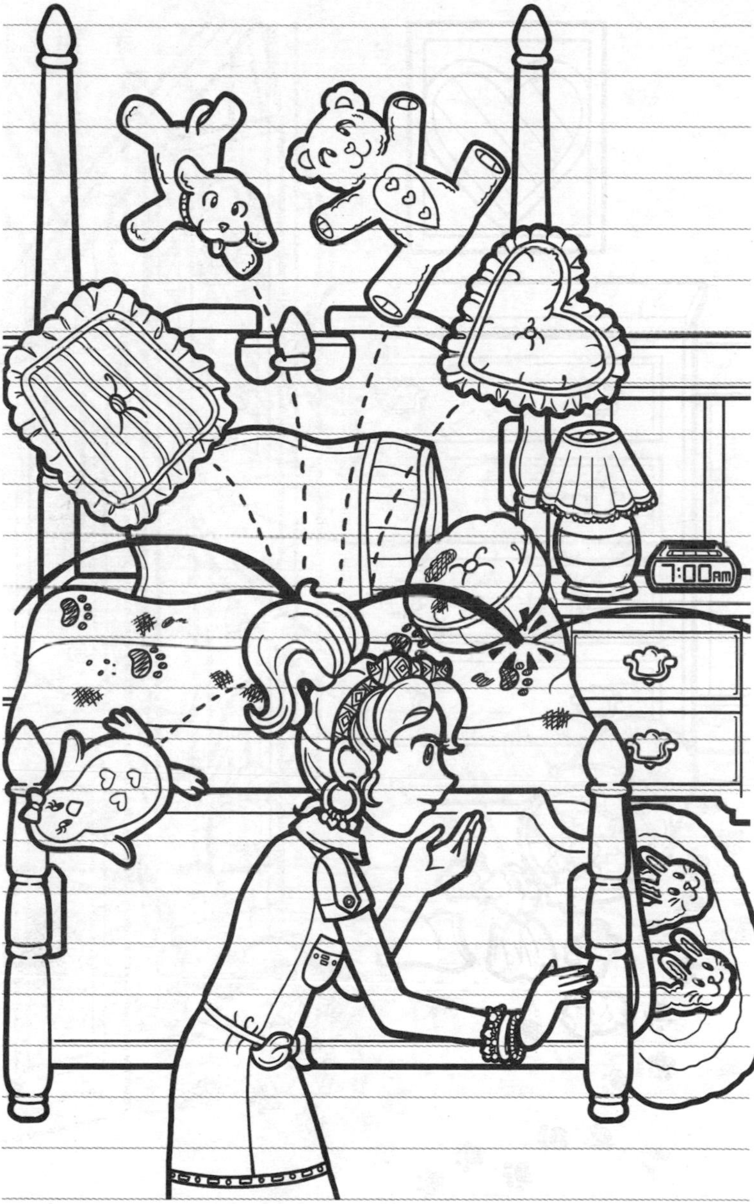
7:00AM

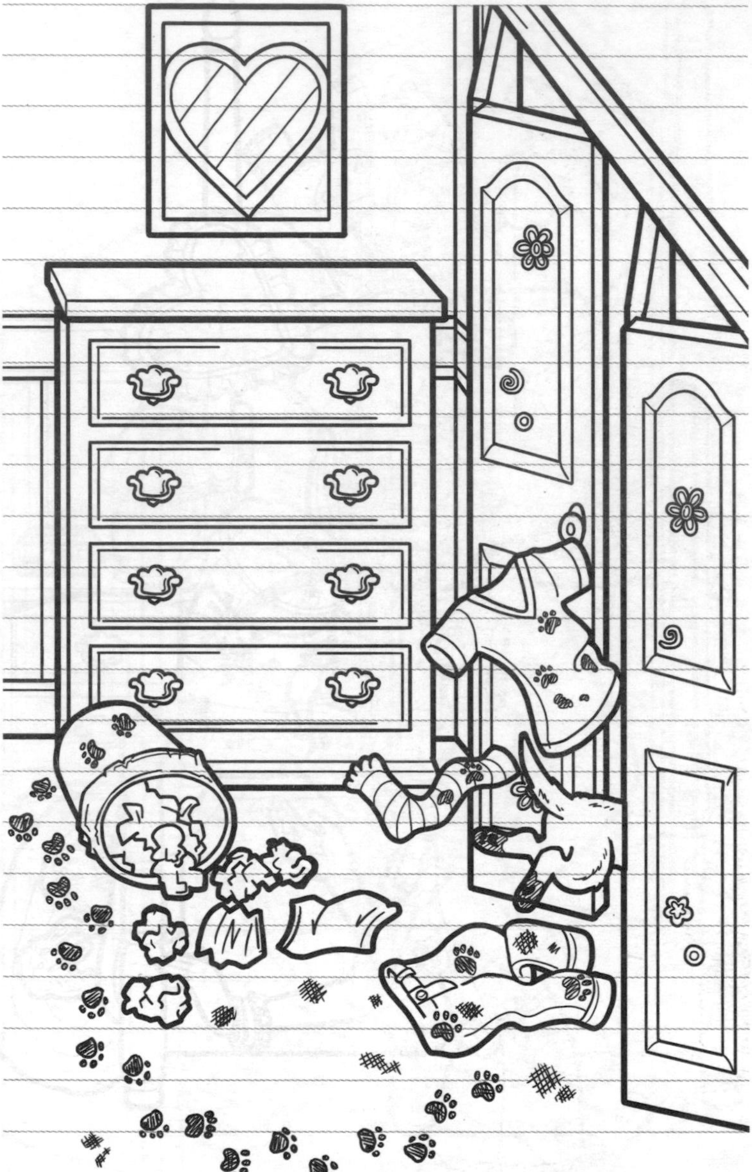

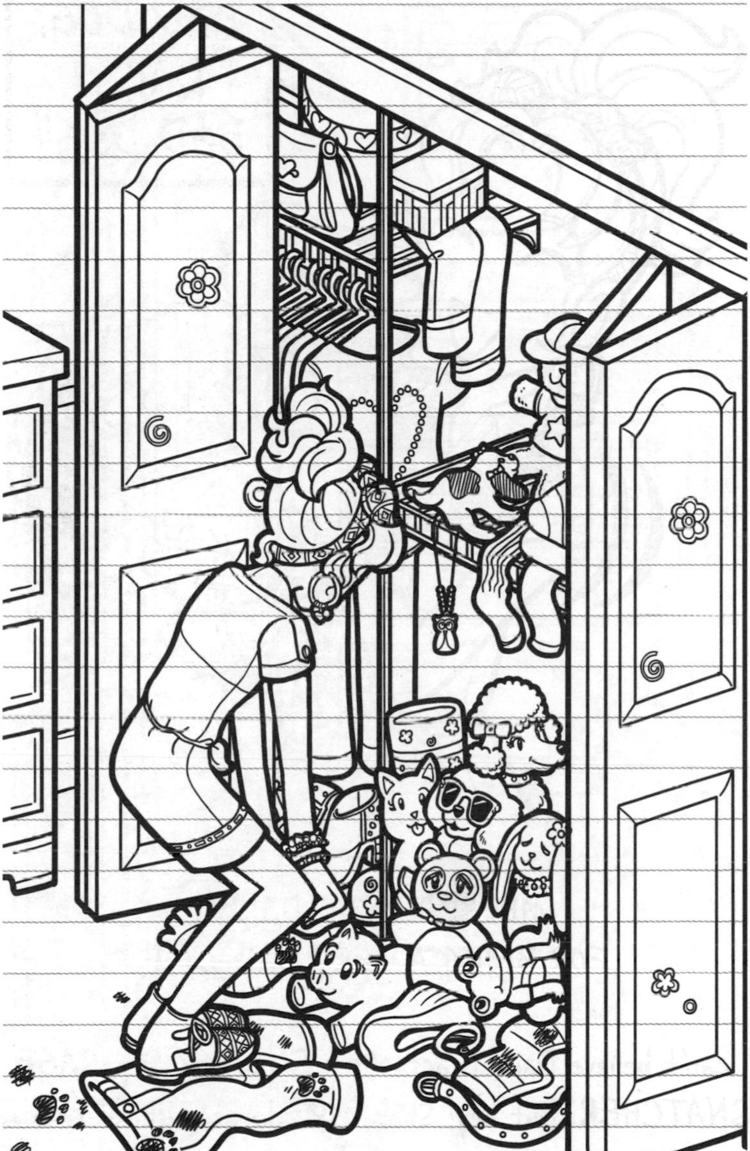

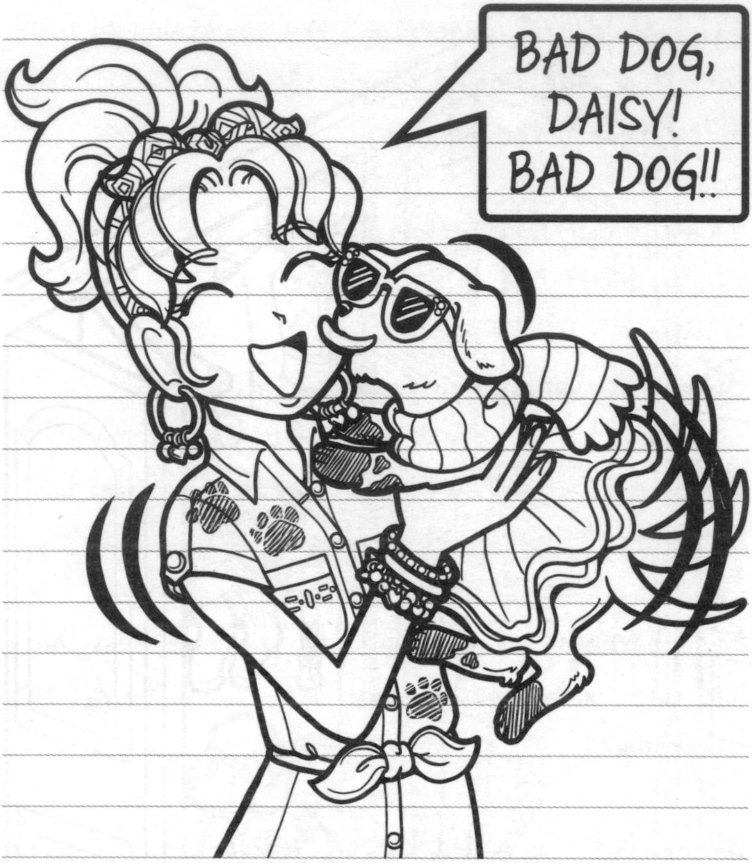
BAD DOG, DAISY! BAD DOG!!

ME, SCOLDING DAISY
FOR BEING A VERY BAD DOG!

I can't believe Daisy is actually a SNEAKY SAUSAGE SNATCHER. But hey! She's *MY* adorable little sneaky sausage snatcher!

I just could NOT understand how something so small, cute, and cuddly could completely TRASH our home in less than three minutes.

There is just ONE major difference between Daisy and my bratty little sister, Brianna.

Brianna is supposed to go potty INSIDE but sometimes has accidents OUTSIDE! And Daisy is supposed to go potty OUTSIDE but sometimes has accidents INSIDE!

I had barely started cleaning up the huge mess Daisy had made when I had to rush her outside to use the bathroom.

Afterward, she waded through a mud puddle and then playfully jumped all over me.

OMG! It looked like Daisy and I had been in a mud-wrestling match. And I had LOST ☹!

I was desperately trying to drag her back into the house when I unexpectedly ran into . . .

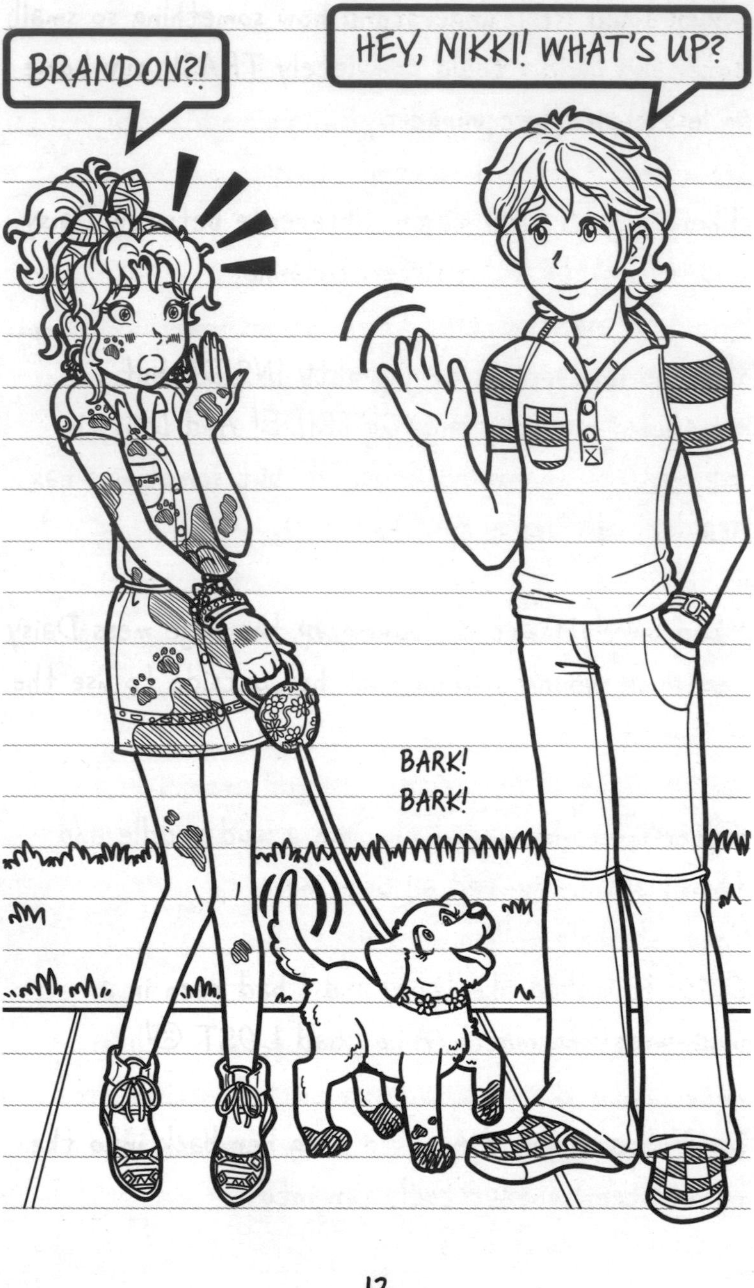
HEY, NIKKI! WHAT'S UP?
BRANDON?!
BARK!
BARK!

OMG! I was SO embarrassed.

I was completely covered in Daisy's muddy paw prints, from head to toe. I wanted to open our mailbox, climb inside it, and DIE!!

Brandon's eyes twinkled as he bit his lower lip. It was quite obvious he was trying his best not to further HUMILIATE me by laughing.

"Um . . . are you okay?" he asked.

"Sure, everything's . . . fine, actually. Daisy and I were just taking a little walk, and . . ."

"Let me guess. You decided to roll around in a mud puddle?" Brandon grinned.

I couldn't help rolling my eyes at him.

Brandon explained that he was up early delivering material to the person designing a donation website for Fuzzy Friends Animal Rescue Center, where he volunteers.

Daisy happily wagged her tail and stared at Brandon like he was a human-sized doggie snack. He scooped her up and laughed. . . .

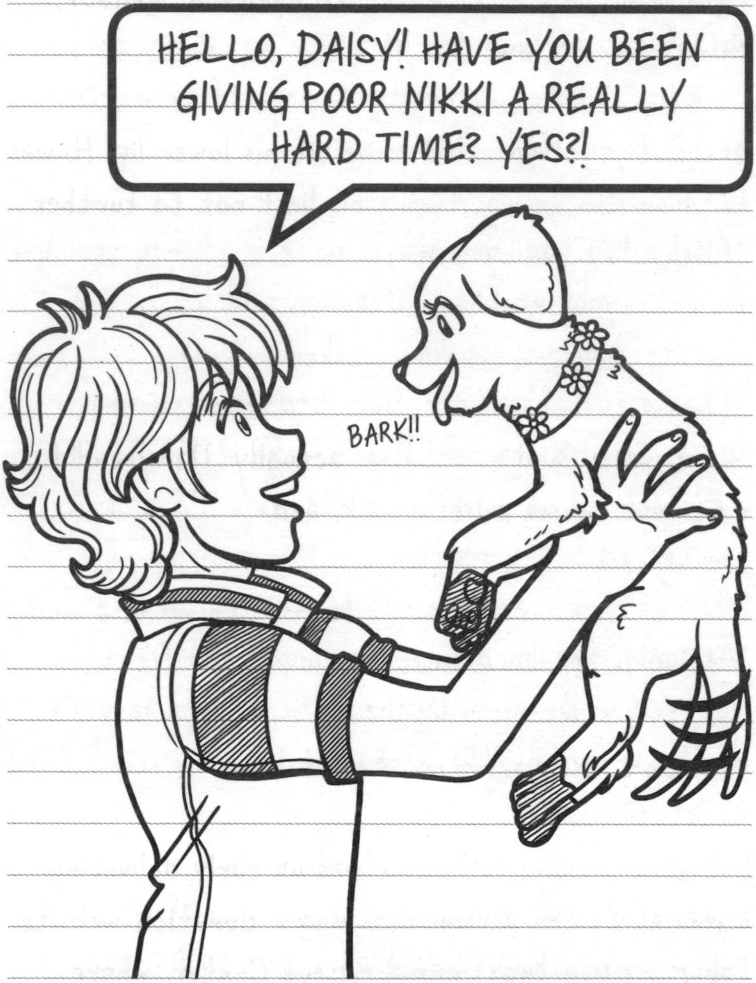
HELLO, DAISY! HAVE YOU BEEN GIVING POOR NIKKI A REALLY HARD TIME? YES?!
BARK!!

BRANDON, CHATTING WITH DAISY

That's when I told him about all the mischief that Daisy had gotten into.

"Brandon, I'm completely exhausted, and I just got out of bed an hour ago. If Daisy was a toy dog, I swear I'd take out her batteries and throw them away!" I grumbled.

"That's too bad. Hey, maybe some obedience training will solve your problem!" Brandon said.

"Thanks for the advice. But obedience training sounds SUPERintense. I barely make it through the TEN minutes of warm-up exercises in PE class," I muttered in frustration.

"Actually, the obedience training is for DAISY. Not YOU!" Brandon laughed. "I'm very sure YOU don't eat out of the garbage or drink out of the toilet. Right?!"

I just stared at Brandon in shock. I could NOT believe he'd actually asked me such a PERSONAL question. How RUDE!!

16

That's when I started to wonder if Brianna had been gossiping about me to Brandon behind my back.

I would NEVER, EVER eat out of the GARBAGE! EWW ☹!

Well, unless I had a REALLY good reason.

Like the time Brianna accidentally threw away the little white bag that contained my double-chocolate, double-fudge cupcake.

I'd actually JUST purchased it from the CupCakery.

YES! I'll admit I had to dig through the garbage to find it.

And there was a big blob of jelly, a half-eaten fish stick, and slimy oatmeal stuck to the outside of the bag that looked pretty nasty.

But the cupcake inside seemed okay, so I actually ATE it. . . .

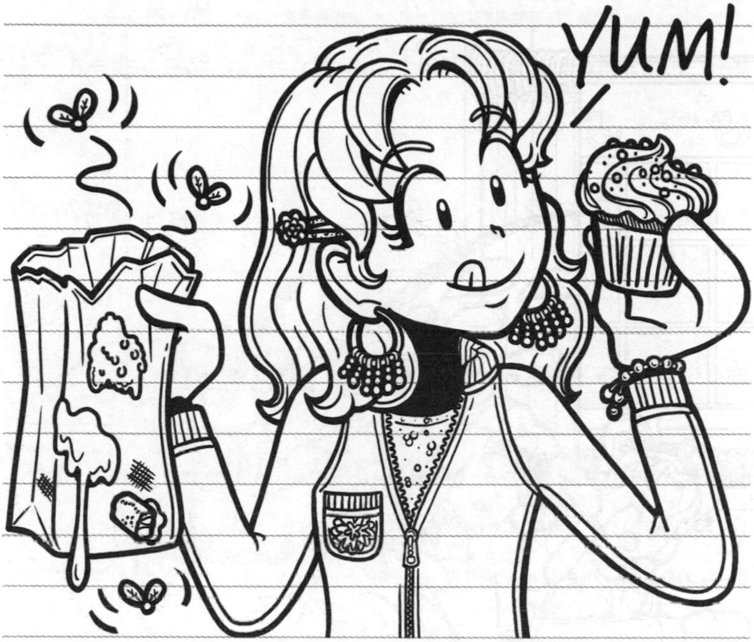
YUM!

ME, EATING OUT OF THE GARBAGE!

I would NEVER, EVER drink anything as gross as TOILET water! EWW ☹!

Well, I wouldn't drink it on purpose, anyway.

A few weeks ago Brianna's teddy bear, Hans, accidentally fell into the toilet. A gallon of toilet water splashed all over me while I was screaming. . . .

ME, SWALLOWING TOILET WATER!

But I DIDN'T have my head stuck inside the toilet bowl, GUZZLING the water like I was dying of thirst or something.

19

I didn't tell Brandon about the garbage or the toilet water because then he'd think I needed doggie obedience training ALONG with Daisy ☹!

Sorry! But I'm a VERY private person, and I don't like putting my business in the streets!

Finally he changed the subject. Thank goodness!

"Listen, Nikki! I have an idea. I'd be happy to train Daisy. We can do two sessions a week, right in your backyard."

"That sounds FANTASTIC!" I exclaimed. "How about Wednesdays and Saturdays, starting this Saturday?"

"No problem! I'm really looking forward to us hanging out. It's going to be fun!"

"Well, Daisy loves hanging out with YOU!" I said.

That's when Brandon STARED right into the . . . murky depths of my . . . inner soul. Then he smiled kind of shy-like and brushed his shaggy bangs out of his eyes. I thought I was going to MELT!

"Actually, I'm looking forward to hanging out with YOU. Not your DOG!" He blushed. . .

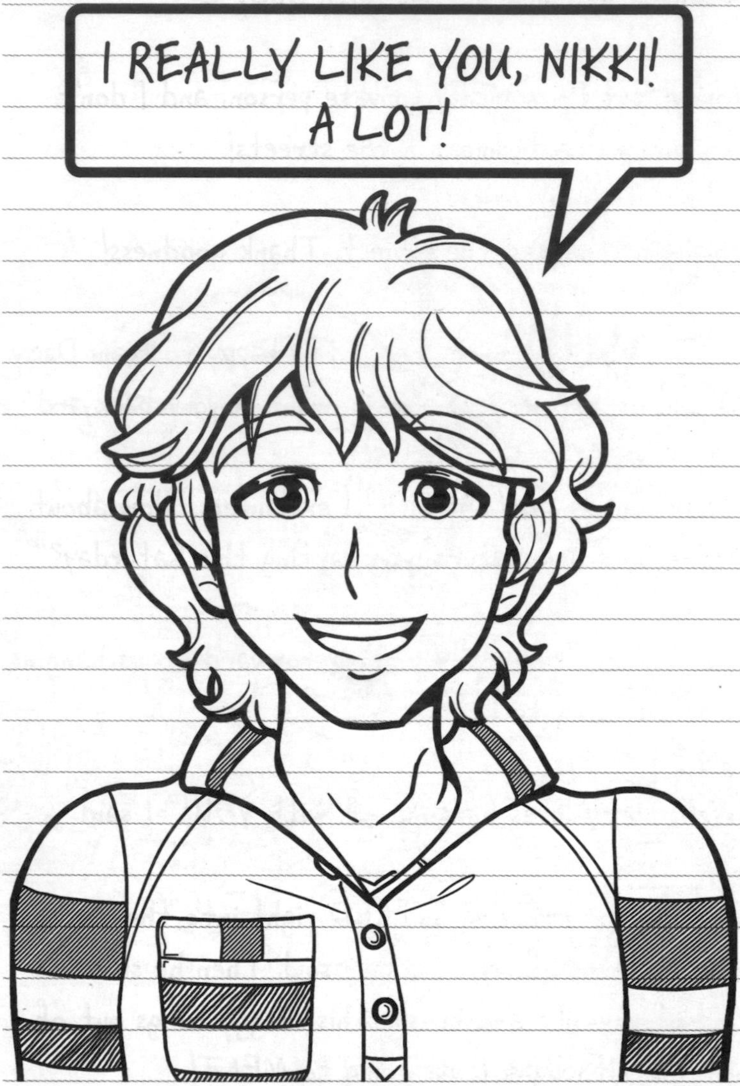
I REALLY LIKE YOU, NIKKI! A LOT!

YES! Brandon actually said those words to me!

SQUEEEEEE ☺!

At that very moment, CRUSH-ITIS hit me!

Like a TON of bricks! . . .

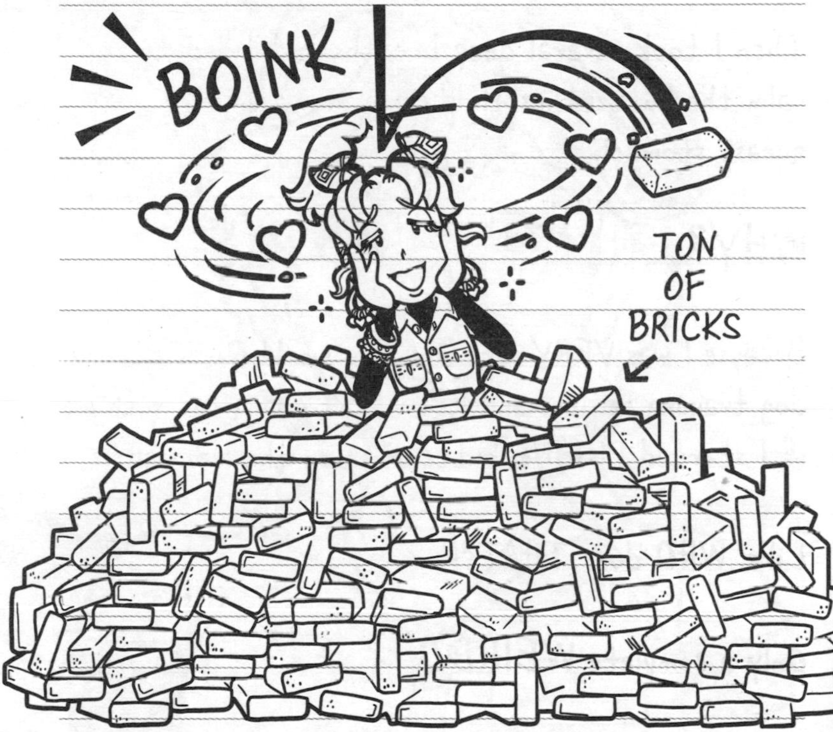
BOINK
TON OF BRICKS

ME, BEING HIT WITH CRUSH-ITIS!

"Um, same here, Brandon," I giggled nervously.
"We're going to have a blast! And by 'we,' I mean
YOU and I. Not my DOG."

"COOL!" Brandon said as he gave me a crooked smile.

"VERY COOL!" I blushed.

Then I took several deep breaths and tried to
calm the butterflies fluttering in my slightly
queasy stomach.

WHY?

Because I was VERY sure Brandon would CANCEL the
dog training sessions and REFUSE to hang out with me
if I started PUKING butterflies on the sidewalk!

Like, WHO does THAT?!!

Only a complete WEIRDO!!

We both just stood there awkwardly smiling at each
other for what seemed like FOREVER!!

Since Brandon had agreed to help me with Daisy, I volunteered to help him with his Fuzzy Friends website project.

He was so happy, he grinned from ear to ear.

So I'll be drawing cute artwork for the website, which we'll be working on mostly at school.

I think Brandon and me spending more time together is a great idea!

Hopefully, we'll become even better friends than we already are.

He likes me a lot and I like him a lot, so WHAT could possibly go WRONG?!

Sorry! But I REFUSE to let anything or anybody RUIN our very special FRIENDSHIP!

Anyway, I really need to stop writing. School starts in less than thirty minutes! And I STILL need to finish cleaning the house and change out of my muddy clothes.

OMG! If my MOM came home from work and saw the HUGE MESS Daisy made, she'd have a complete MELTDOWN.

She'd drop Daisy and me off at Fuzzy Friends . . .

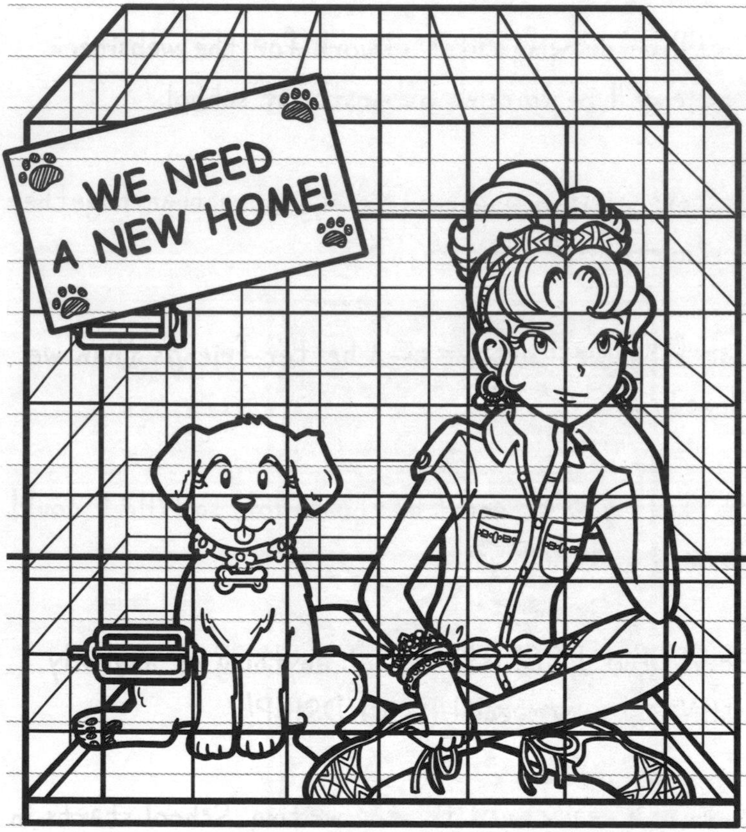
WE NEED A NEW HOME!

. . . TO BE ADOPTED BY A NEW FAMILY!!

I can't wait to tell my BFFs, Chloe and Zoey, the very exciting news that Brandon and I will be hanging out together training Daisy AND working on his Fuzzy Friends project.

And since Chloe reads a lot of teen romance and Zoey is into self-help books, I'm sure they'll give me advice on how to deal with my CRUSH-ITIS!

WOW! I just had the STRANGEST thought! I wonder if it's CONTAGIOUS?! . . .

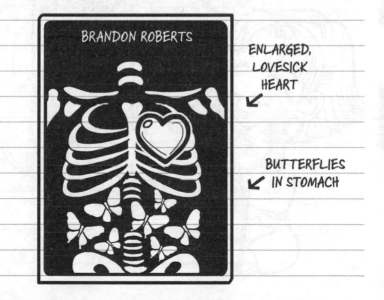

BRANDON ROBERTS

ENLARGED, LOVESICK HEART

BUTTERFLIES IN STOMACH

YOU NEVER KNOW!! ☺!!

THURSDAY, MAY 22—9:45 A.M.
AT MY LOCKER

Yesterday during lunch I confided in Chloe and Zoey about my crush-itis and everything that had happened between Brandon and me.

They were VERY supportive and gave me a great big HUG! . . .

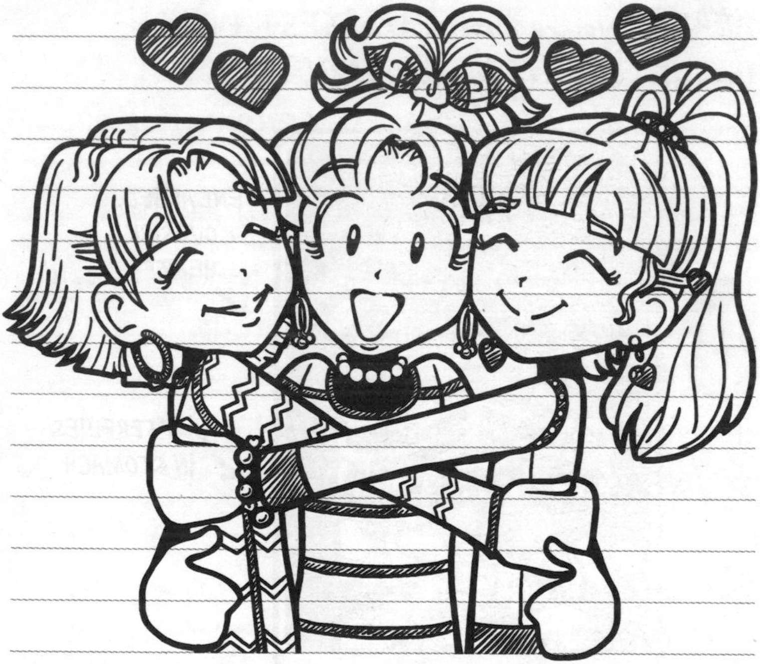

CHLOE, ZOEY, AND I DO A GROUP HUG!!

"Nikki, you have more ISSUES than a two-year subscription to *Seventeen* magazine!" Chloe teased.

"But we still LOVE you!" Zoey giggled.

Chloe and Zoey are practically EXPERTS on teen romance and gave me some awesome advice. . . .

First of all, a CRUSH can be a noun (the PERSON you're obsessed with) or a verb (having warm-'n'-fuzzy FEELINGS for that person). Which means you can CRUSH on your CRUSH ☺!

It's also perfectly normal to feel NERVOUS and a little AWKWARD around your crush.

Heck, I get NERVOUS just THINKING ABOUT how NERVOUS Brandon makes me feel!

But here's the really crazy part. Because you're a NERVOUS WRECK, you'll often SAY and DO incredibly STUPID and EMBARRASSING things that make your crush-itis even WORSE. . . .

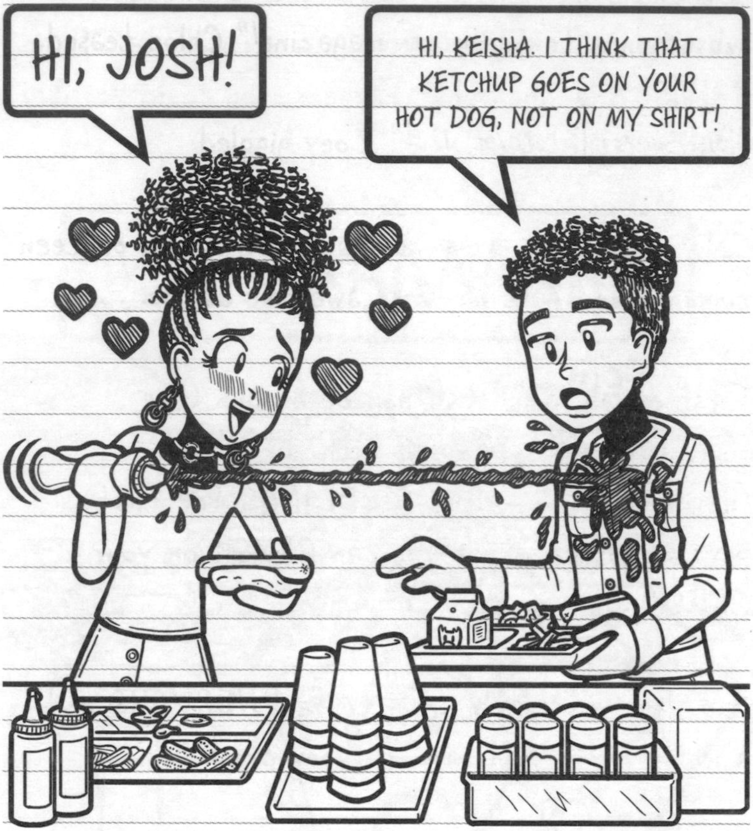
HI, JOSH!
HI, KEISHA. I THINK THAT KETCHUP GOES ON YOUR HOT DOG, NOT ON MY SHIRT!

HOW TO COMPLETELY HUMILIATE YOURSELF IN FRONT OF YOUR CRUSH!

The GOOD NEWS is that the whole crush thing is mostly just harmless fun ☺! Your crush will probably NEVER even know you're actually crushing on 'em.

But the BAD NEWS is that even the mildest crush can potentially evolve into a CRUSH-ITIS CRISIS! And when that happens, you could possibly LOSE. YOUR. MIND!! . . .

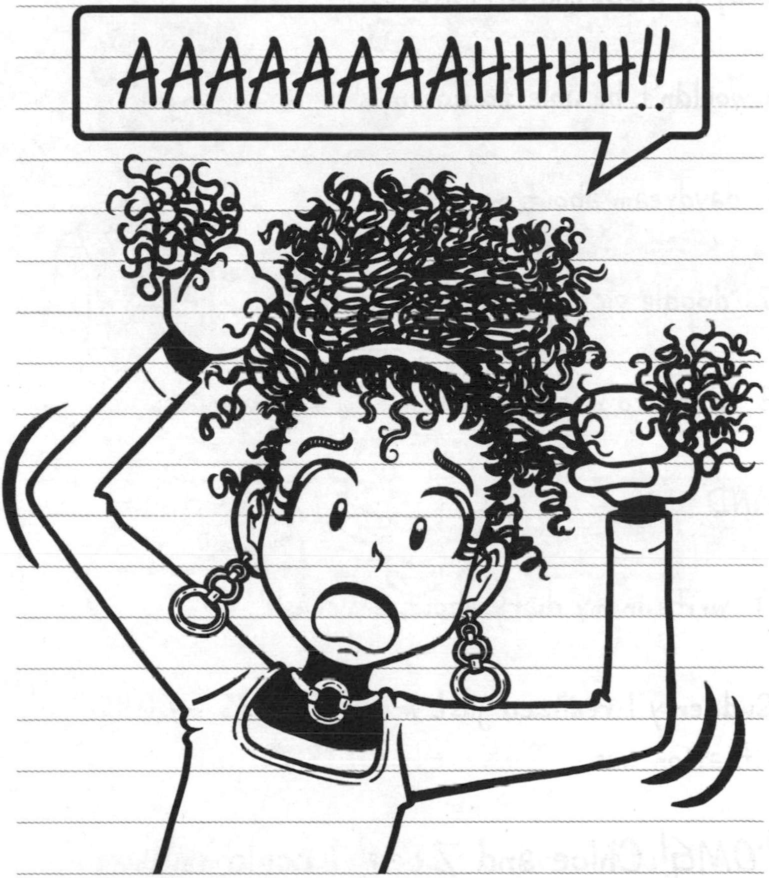
AAAAAAAAHHHH!!

A CLASSIC CRUSH ESCALATING INTO A CRUSH-ITIS CRISIS!

The SCARIEST part for me is that if my crush-itis gets worse, I could end up missing school!

And what if it gets to the point where I have to stay in BED the ENTIRE summer?!

I wouldn't be able to do anything except . . .

1. daydream about my crush

2. doodle pictures of my crush

3. listen to music that reminds me of my crush

AND

4. write in my diary about my crush.

Suddenly I realized just how SERIOUS my situation was.

"OMG! Chloe and Zoey! I could end up bedridden and suffering from CRUSH-ITIS for the rest of my LIFE!!" . . .

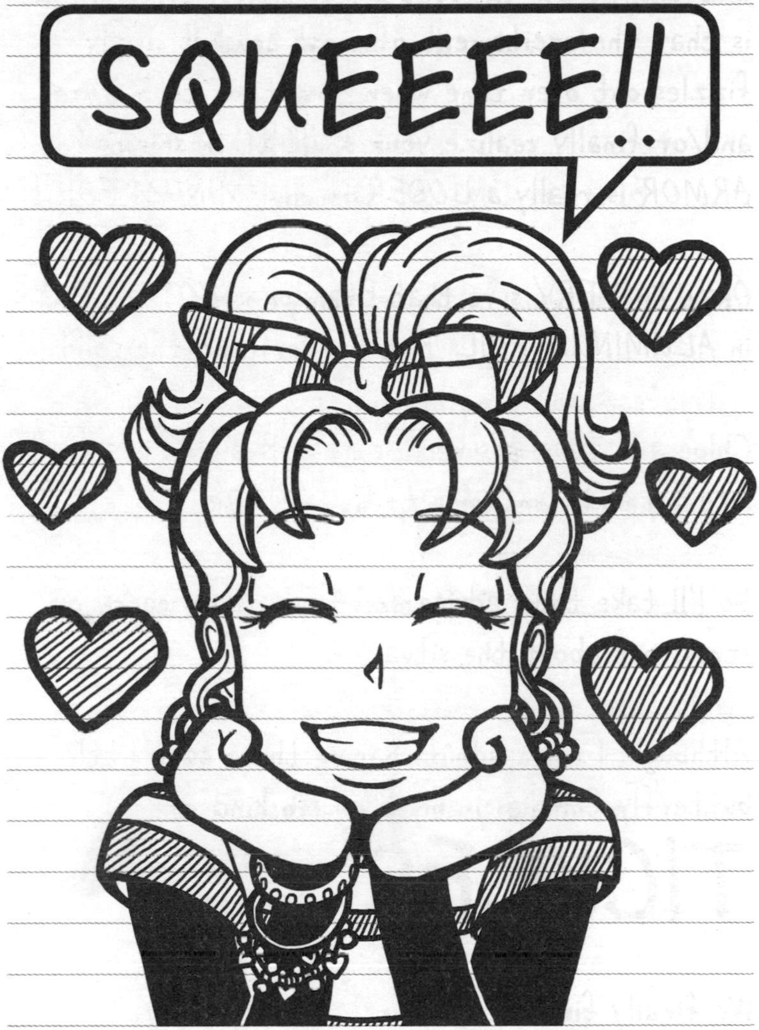
SQUEEEE!!

ME, FEELING INSANELY HAPPY AND WISHING THAT MY CRUSH-ITIS LASTS FOREVER!!

But the most important thing I need to remember is that the excitement of most crushes simply fizzles out over time when you start to mature and/or finally realize your KNIGHT in shining ARMOR is really a LOSER in ALUMINUM FOIL!

Okay, I'm VERY sure that Brandon is NOT a LOSER in ALUMINUM FOIL. But I understand the point.

Chloe and Zoey assured me that Brandon is a really nice guy and I am going to be just fine.

So I'll take their advice and try not to worry or stress out about the situation.

Although, I must admit, having those cute little butterfly thingies in my stomach kind of

TICKLES!

We finally finished our lunch, and then my BFFs did the SWEETEST thing. They treated me to an extra-large HOT FUDGE BROWNIE SUNDAE from the snack bar!

And when I asked why they were being so kind to me, Zoey broke into giggles and exclaimed . . .

"Actually, we're saving all our money for our summer tour. And buying you ice cream is CHEAPER than THERAPY!!"

You gotta LOVE 'em!!

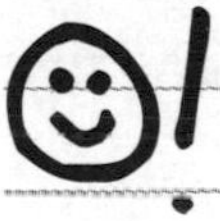

FRIDAY, MAY 23—2:30 P.M.
AT MY LOCKER

I can't believe school will be over in a little more than a week. SQUEEEEEEEE ☺!!

Even though the entire year has been a nonstop DRAMAFEST, it actually went by pretty fast.

Summer vacation is going to be a total BLAST!!

In July my band, Actually, I'm Not Really Sure Yet, will be doing a monthlong national tour as the opening act for the superstar boy band . . .

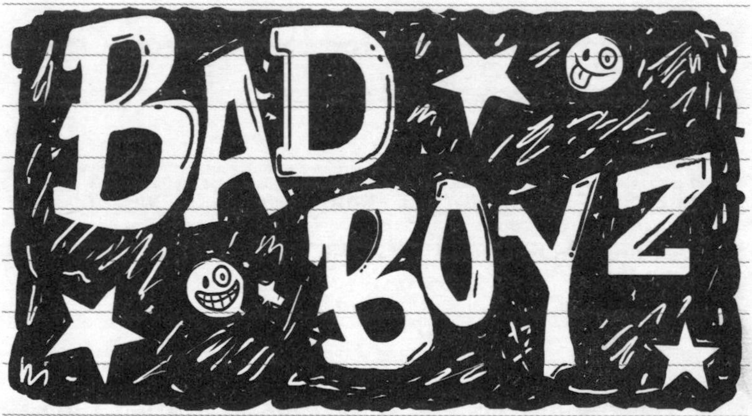
BAD
BOYZ

How COOL and EXCITING will that be ☺?!!

Trevor Chase, the world-famous producer, has asked me to put together a thirty-minute show that includes our original song "Dorks Rule!"

We'll officially start band rehearsals again after the school year ends. OMG! I can't even imagine going on a national tour with BRANDON ☺! And the rest of my band members too!

Chloe and Zoey are SUPERexcited about our tour and have been talking about it nonstop. They also plan to post videos on YouTube of their tour adventures in hopes of landing their own reality TV show.

They already have a name for their project: *Chloe and Zoey: Teens on Tour!*

As their BFF, the LAST thing I wanted was to discourage them from pursuing their dream of having a TV show.

But after doing my own show back in March, I am so OVER reality TV! . . .

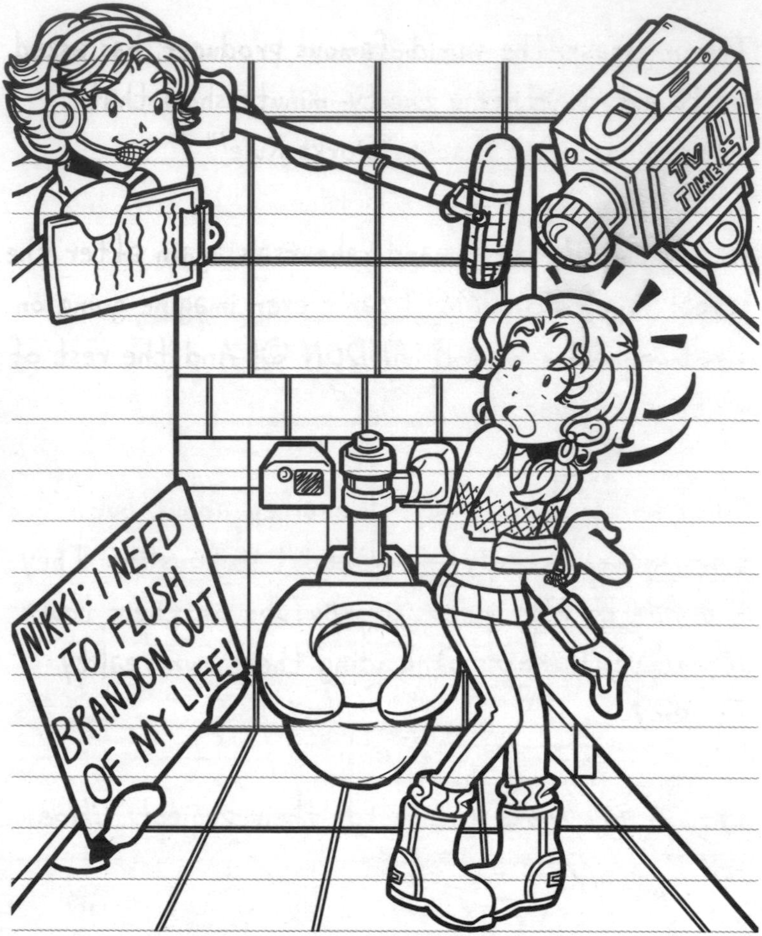
TV TIME!
NIKKI: I NEED TO FLUSH BRANDON OUT OF MY LIFE!

ME, FREAKING OUT ABOUT
THE TV CAMERAS EVERYWHERE ☹!

I'm helping Chloe and Zoey brainstorm ideas for their show, and I'll try to be supportive of them from BEHIND the camera.

I ALSO applied for a scholarship to study abroad in PARIS, FRANCE, this summer ☺!

OMG! Can you imagine ME touring the city and hanging out at the famous Louvre art museum? . . .

BONJOUR!
PARIS BOUND
TRES
BON!

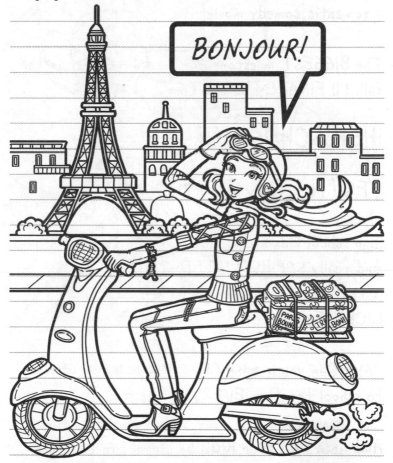

ME, SPENDING THE SUMMER IN PARIS!

I know! To be honest, NEITHER can I ☹!

So I'm definitely NOT going to sit around holding my BREATH, waiting for a FANTASY SUMMER IN PARIS to happen. WHY? Because LIFE is NOT a romantic comedy movie!

The BIGGEST milestone for me will be that in the fall, I'll FINALLY be starting . . .

HIGH SCHOOL ☺!!

YES!! I'll actually be a FRESHMAN!

High school kids are so COOL. And very MATURE. And really SOPHISTICATED! The BEST thing is that they're old enough to get a DRIVER'S LICENSE!

OMG! Can you imagine Chloe, Zoey, and me driving to school together EVERY. SINGLE. DAY?!

And since we'll be in HIGH SCHOOL, we'll be very cool, mature, and sophisticated TOO!!

I bet we'll be so different then that we'll BARELY recognize ourselves in the mirror! Or in a really CUTE hot pink sporty convertible! . . .

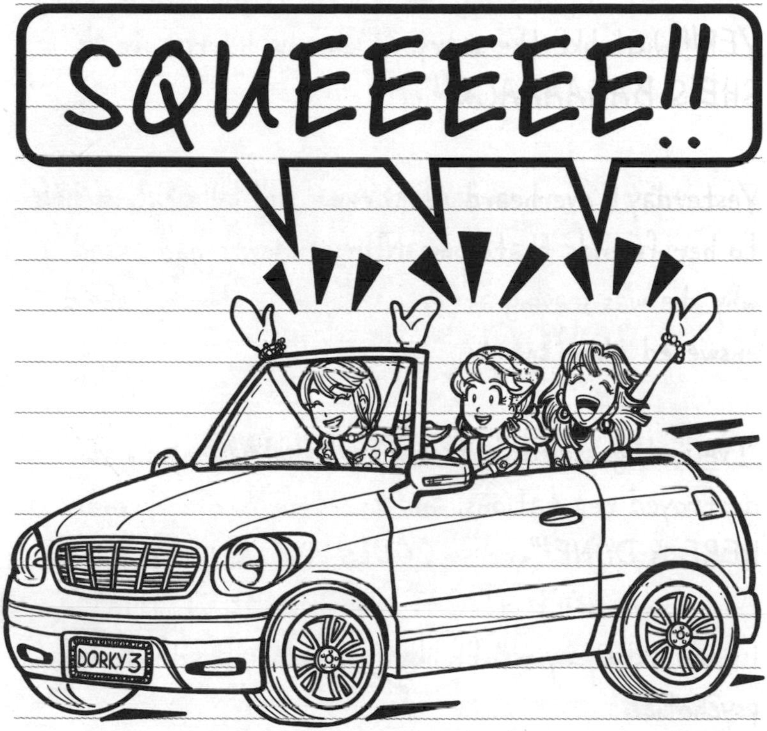
SQUEEEEE!!
DORKY 3

CHLOE, ZOEY, AND ME IN HIGH SCHOOL!

The best thing about high school is that I WON'T have a locker next to MacKenzie Hollister anymore. Thank goodness ☺!

Did I mention that MacKenzie transferred from North Hampton Hills BACK to Westchester Country Day on Tuesday?!

YEP!! Just like the scary villain in a horror movie . . . SHE'S BAAAAAACK!!

Yesterday I overheard MacKenzie actually BRAGGING to her friends that some NHH students had asked why she was leaving after barely a month and she'd answered them smugly . . .

"I've lied, gossiped, backstabbed, started nasty rumors, destroyed reputations, and created chaos. My work HERE is DONE!"

I mean, WHO says stuff like that? Only a self-absorbed, psychotic . . .

SOCIOPATH!!

Calling MacKenzie a MEAN GIRL is an understatement. She's PURE EVIL in hair extensions and sparkly nail polish.

When life gives MacKenzie LEMONS, she MALICIOUSLY squirts the juice in other people's EYES! . . .

MACKENZIE SHOWS OFF HER SKILLZ
WITH FRESH LEMONS!

I had just arrived at my first-hour class when I was handed a note from the OFFICE.

Of course I was VERY worried. MacKenzie had recently tried to get me kicked out of school on a

phony allegation of cyberbullying. It was very possible that she was stirring up MORE drama.

Or maybe the school janitor had FINALLY figured out that my BFFs and I had been SECRETLY hanging out in his janitor's closet for the past NINE MONTHS.

We could be facing a week of detention ☹!

Anyway, after talking to the secretary, I received some surprising news.

Our school is hosting students for another week of the student exchange program with local schools, and I've been drafted to be a student ambassador. JUST GREAT ☹!

I actually participated in this SAME program a week ago at North Hampton Hills International Academy. It was supposed to be the last week, but apparently the program was so popular that it was extended so more kids from other schools could participate.

Unfortunately, my student ambassador was a

selfie-addicted drama queen named Tiffany.

OMG! The girl was TREACHEROUS! She made MacKenzie look like Dora the Explorer! . . .

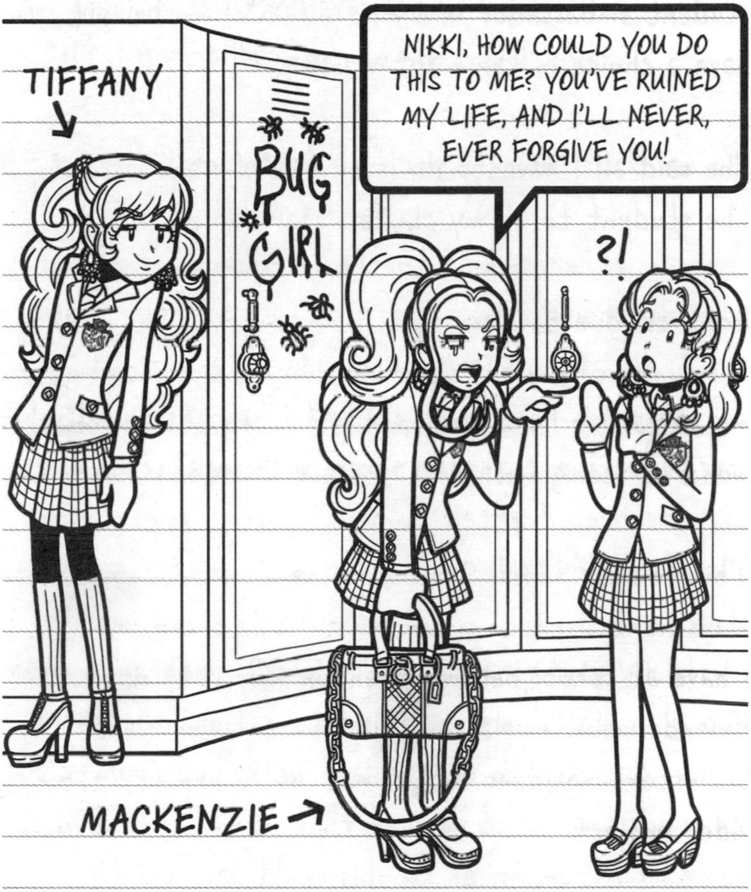
TIFFANY
NIKKI, HOW COULD YOU DO THIS TO ME? YOU'VE RUINED MY LIFE, AND I'LL NEVER, EVER FORGIVE YOU!
BUG GIRL
?!
MACKENZIE

TIFFANY VANDALIZES MACKENZIE'S LOCKER AND FRAMES ME FOR IT!!

I'd LOVE to tell you all the dirty details, but THAT is another DIARY.

Anyway, the secretary said my participation as a student ambassador is MANDATORY! So I don't have a choice in the matter ☹!

She said all I have to do is be friendly and escort the student to all my classes, starting on Monday.

However, due to class sizes, she temporarily switched the times of my PE class and library hour, and gave me an earlier lunch period. So it looks like I probably won't be seeing much of Chloe and Zoey next week ☹.

This totally STINKS because I've ALREADY made plans next week to spend what little spare time I have at school helping Brandon with his Fuzzy Friends website, planning our concert tour, and brainstorming ideas with Chloe and Zoey for their video project.

Anyway, the school secretary told me the exchange student's name and gave me an e-mail address.

I think she said it was Angie.

No, it was . . . Andrea.

I think.

I just hope she's nice.

Between the exchange student, Daisy's training, Brandon's Fuzzy Friends project, the summer tour, AND my BFFs' YouTube videos, my schedule for the end of school is going to be . . .

BRUTAL

But, luckily, my CRUSH and BFFs are very understanding and SUPERsupportive!

So WHAT could possibly go WRONG?!

☺‼

Chloe and Zoey came over after school. We ordered pizza and hung out.

I confessed to my BFFs that after all the senseless DRAMA with Tiffany at NHH, I was a little worried about spending an entire week with Andrea.

I mean, WHAT if Tiffany and Andrea were friends?!

Andrea could be a selfie-addicted drama queen too!

Chloe and Zoey came up with an idea that was pure GENIUS!

They said it might help if I sent a friendly e-mail to Andrea introducing myself BEFORE we officially meet on Monday.

So that's exactly what I did. . . .

* * * * * * * * * * * * * *

Hi,

My name is Nikki, and I'm going to be your student
ambassador at Westchester Country Day. I'm
looking forward to meeting you on Monday. If
you have any questions, just let me know and I'll
be happy to answer them (as long as they're NOT
about geometry homework). Take care 😊!

Nikki

* * * * * * * * * * * * * *

As soon as I hit the send button, I immediately
started to have second thoughts.

What if Andrea thought my e-mail was silly and
that I was really immature for my age ☹?!

I was surprised when about fifteen minutes later
an e-mail from Andrea popped into my inbox. Wow!
That was FAST!

48

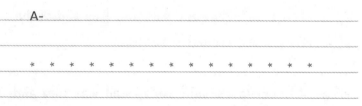

* * * * * * * * * * * * * * *

Hi, Nikki,

Thanks for the e-mail. I'm really looking forward to meeting you, too.

To be quite honest, I'm a little nervous about spending the week at WCD. And I'm even more nervous about pop quizzes in geometry!

Any advice or tips you could give me about fitting in at WCD and NOT completely HUMILIATING myself would be greatly appreciated.

A-

* * * * * * * * * * * * * * *

Hi, A-,

Don't worry! Like at most schools, the majority of students at WCD are pretty nice. Just avoid the mean girls and the super-annoying guys and you'll

be fine. None of the guys have made fun of my hairy legs. Lately 😊!

I can't wait for you to meet my BFFs, Chloe and Zoey. And Brandon, too. He's my crush and a TOTAL CUTIE! You can just call us Branikki! But PLEASE don't tell him I said that (LOL). We'll all be hanging out together. It's going to be fun 😊!

Nikki

* * * * * * * * * * * * * * *

Hi, Nikki,

Thanks for the advice. I feel a lot better already. I'm glad you're my student ambassador.

I just transferred to NHH a few weeks ago, so I haven't made any friends here yet. You're lucky to have friends like Chloe, Zoey, and Brandon. I can't wait to meet all of you.

A-

* * * * * * * * * * * * * * * *

Hi, A-,

Being the new kid totally sucks! Been there, done
that, got the T-shirt!

I was recently at NHH for this same program, so
we may have even passed each other in the halls.
I met some nice kids there and made a lot of new
friends. You should definitely consider joining the
NHH Science Club! We'll talk more when you get
here. Have a great weekend 😊!

Nikki

* * * * * * * * * * * * * * * *

Chloe and Zoey's idea worked like a charm!

After our e-mails, it almost feels like Andrea and I
already know each other.

She seems really nice and has a wacky sense of humor.

51

I can't wait to introduce her to the NHH Science Club members.

To give Andrea a really warm welcome, I came up with the COOLEST idea.

I made a welcome sign out of hot pink glitter.

I think she's going to LOVE it! . . .

WELCOME,
ANDREA,
TO WCD!!

Well, at least Andrea is NOT a self-absorbed, psychotic SOCIOPATH (like some people I know).

Okay, I'll admit I was wrong!

It looks like this student ambassador thing is NOT going to be a major PAIN IN THE BEHIND after all.

It's going to be FUN!

And I might end up making a REALLY good friend!

☺!!

SATURDAY, MAY 24—NOON
IN MY BACKYARD

Today was Daisy's first doggie obedience session with Brandon, and I could hardly wait.

Since he volunteers several times a week at Fuzzy Friends, he's an excellent dog trainer. I had no doubt that very soon Daisy was going to be the best-trained dog in the entire city.

I was even thinking about entering her in one of those SUPERfancy dog shows. You know, where snobby people prance around with their snobby dogs in front of a snobby judge and the winner gets a big trophy.

In a few months, THAT could be US!

SQUEEEEEEEE ☺!

And Brandon will there with Daisy and me to capture it all. . . .

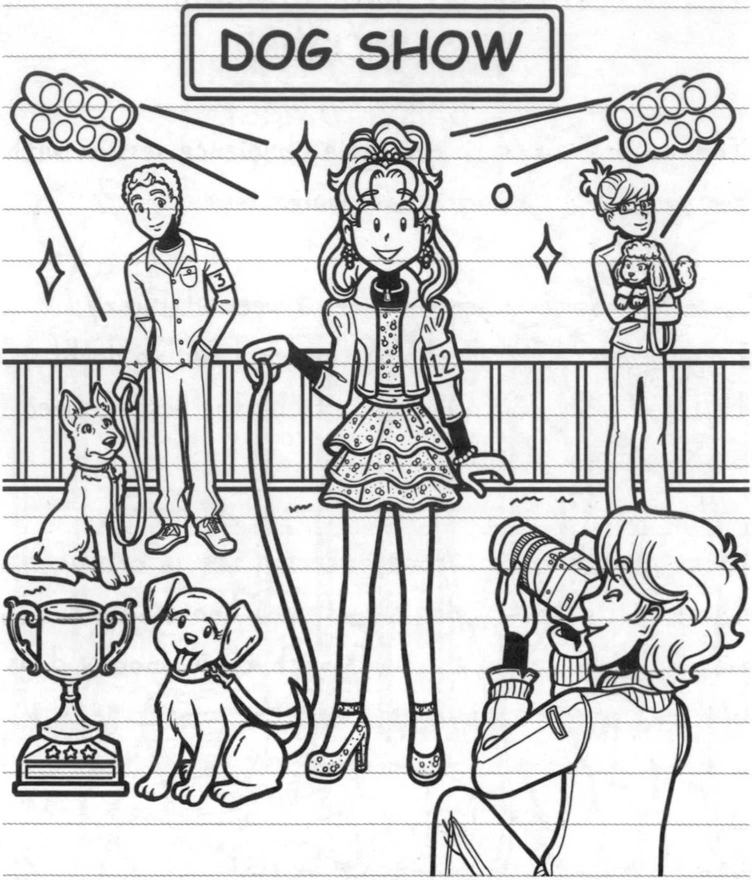
DOG SHOW

DAISY WINS BEST IN SHOW!!

Daisy and I sat in the backyard and listened carefully as Brandon enthusiastically explained her first lesson. . .

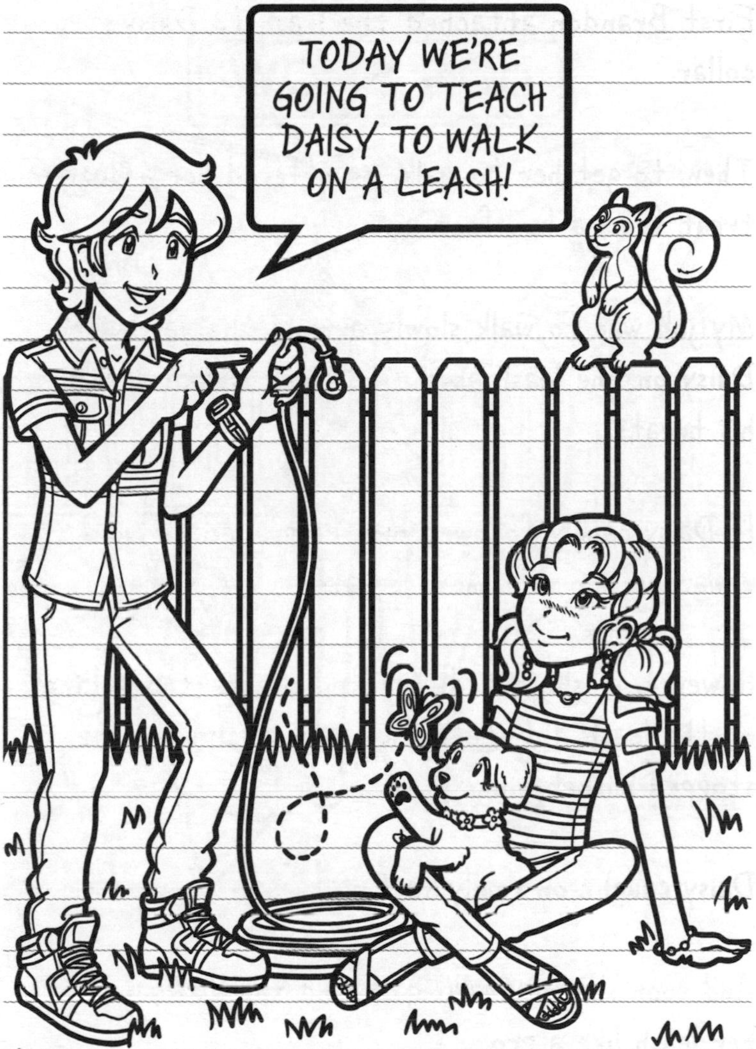
TODAY WE'RE GOING TO TEACH DAISY TO WALK ON A LEASH!

DAISY'S FIRST TRAINING SESSION WITH BRANDON!

First Brandon attached the leash to Daisy's collar.

Then, to get her to walk, he offered her a doggie treat from a few feet away.

My job was to walk slowly around the yard with Daisy on the leash as she followed Brandon and his treats.

If Daisy calmly followed him, he praised her and rewarded her with more treats.

However, if she got distracted or started pulling on the leash, I'd stand firmly in place until she stopped misbehaving.

Daisy caught on really fast.

And soon she was walking around the backyard on her leash like a pro.

Until she got bored and decided it would be more fun to hang out with a SQUIRREL. . . .

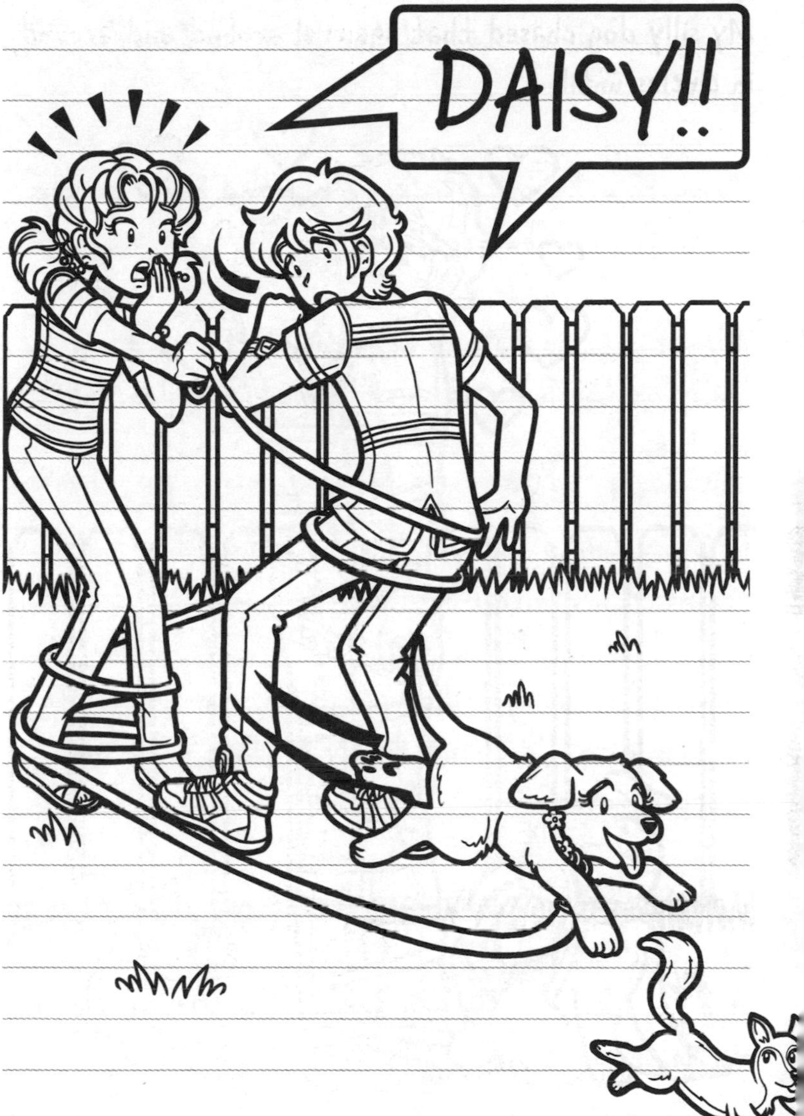
DAISY!!

DAISY, TRYING TO MAKE FRIENDS WITH A SQUIRREL

My silly dog chased that squirrel around and around in circles until . . .

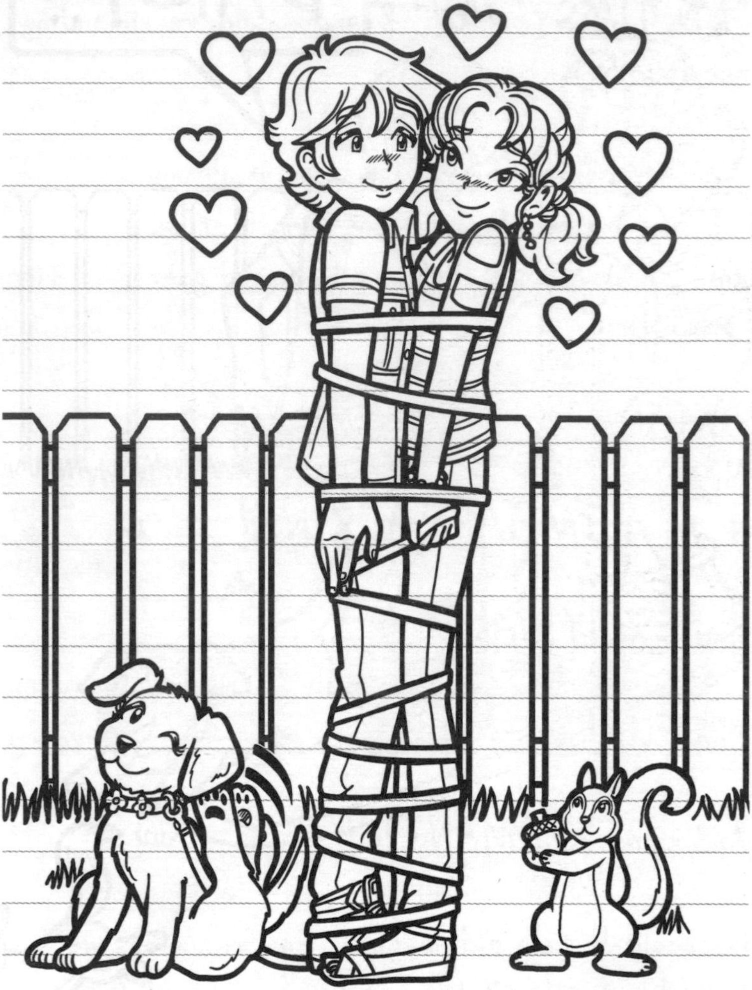

BRANDON AND I FOUND OURSELVES A LITTLE, UM . . . TANGLED UP!!

"BAD DOG, DAISY! BAD DOG!" I yelled.

"NO, DAISY! NO!" Brandon said, reprimanding her sternly.

But she just sat there, staring at us all innocent-like with her big brown puppy-dog eyes, pretending she didn't have the slightest idea how we'd gotten all tied up like that.

OMG!

It was so EMBARRASSING!

And EXCITING!

And FUN!

And kind of ROMANTIC!

We couldn't help but laugh at how ridiculous we looked as we tried to untangle ourselves from Daisy's leash.

In spite of the squirrel FIASCO, we both agreed that Daisy is a smart dog and had successfully learned to walk on a leash.

At our next session Brandon will be teaching Daisy the sit and stay commands.

I just hope it will be as ~~fun and romantic~~ interesting and educational as today's lesson was.

SQUEEEEEE!!

!!

SATURDAY—3:00 P.M.
IN MY BEDROOM

After Brandon left, I decided to finish up my history homework.

I was in my bedroom when someone knocked on my door. I assumed it was Brianna.

"No, Brianna! You can't play the Princess Sugar Plum video game on my cell phone!" I yelled. "I'm doing my homework!"

My dad opened the door and stuck his head in. "Nikki, it's me. I need to be on the social medium," he announced. "Can you help me?"

"The social medium? Dad, what are you talking about?!" I asked.

"You know, the Instachat, the Snapgram, the Facefriends, and Tweetering! I want it all for my business, Maxwell's Bug Extermination!" he said, sitting down on my bed. UNINVITED!! . . .

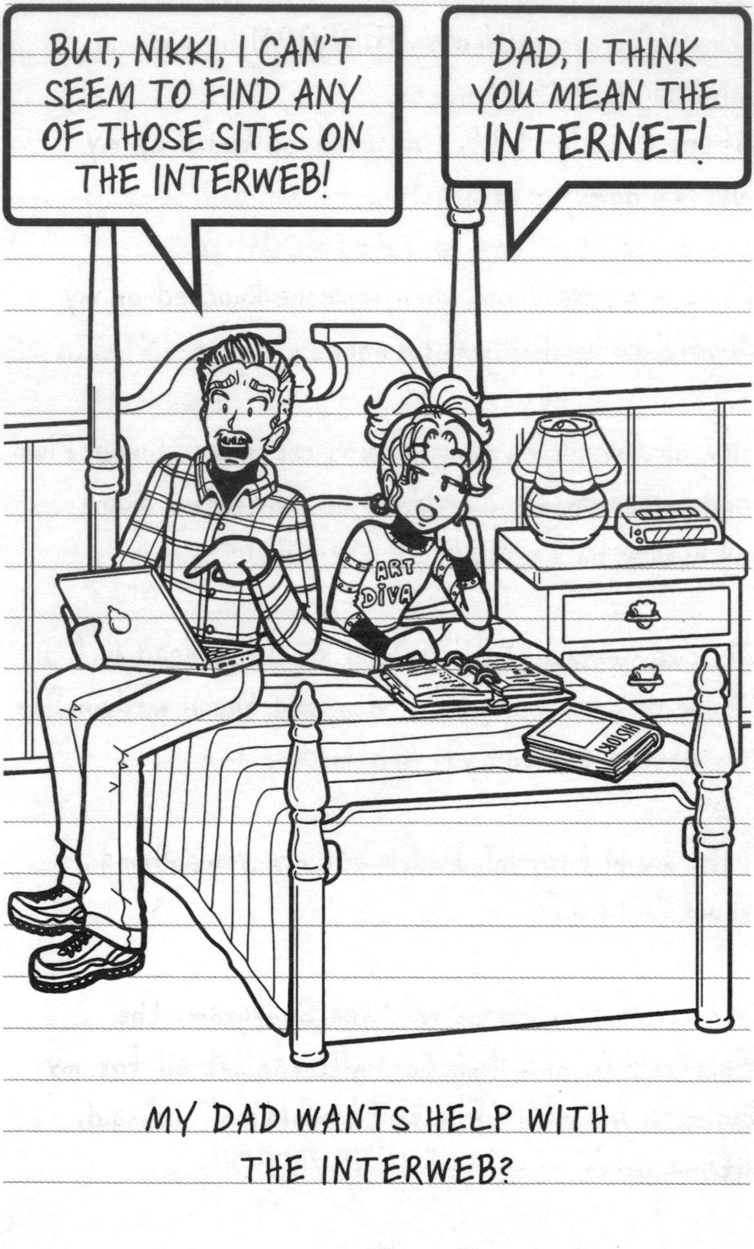
BUT, NIKKI, I CAN'T SEEM TO FIND ANY OF THOSE SITES ON THE INTERWEB!
DAD, I THINK YOU MEAN THE INTERNET!
ART DIVA
HISTORY

MY DAD WANTS HELP WITH THE INTERWEB?

My mom is on Facebook, keeping up with her high school friends and embarrassing ME by posting UNAUTHORIZED photos.

But my dad? He still listens to baseball games on an old-school, battery-operated BOOM BOX.

"I need to be on the Interweb, er, I mean, INTERNET, to get more business," he explained. "I want to sign up for all those popular sites, like Bookface and Instagrammy. I need to be connected and keep my finger on the pulse of the youth."

The way my dad had MURDERED the names of all those social media sites, I doubted there was a pulse. No wonder he couldn't find them online.

I set my history homework aside and grabbed his computer.

He watched as I googled "popular media sites" and then clicked on a link to a website. Within seconds a list appeared with links to all the popular sites he had mangled.

"There you go, Dad," I said, handing his computer back to him.

"Thanks, Nikki!" He beamed. "I really appreciate your help. As a matter of fact, I'd like you to have these!"

He took out his wallet and handed me what I thought at first were dollar bills ☺! Only it wasn't money. It was gift cards ☹. Four "Big Bucks" gift cards to Queasy Cheesy pizza parlor, to be exact: "Good for one FREE pizza and large soda on Saturdays 1:00–3:00 p.m."

"Thanks, Dad." I smiled.

I had a hunch he might have gotten the gift cards from the owner after exterminating the place. But since I might actually be EATING there, I didn't want to know the dirty details.

I guess I could always sell the gift cards on the INTERWEB for some cold cash. Right, Dad?!

☺!!

SUNDAY, MAY 25—4:30 P.M.
IN MY BEDROOM

Today it was raining like crazy! Which meant
I was trapped inside the house with my NUTTY
family ☹!

I decided to spend some quality time lounging in
bed, writing in my diary (about you-know-who!)
while nibbling on chocolate.

So I brought out my secret stash of candy ☺!

I actually had to keep it hidden or Brianna
would gobble up every last piece in less than sixty
seconds.

Hey! I've seen her do it!

TWICE ☹!

I guess Mom wanted to take full advantage of the
rainy day. So she decided we needed to have some
Family Sharing Time.

"Now it's time for Board Game Madness!" she announced cheerfully as we finished lunch. . . .

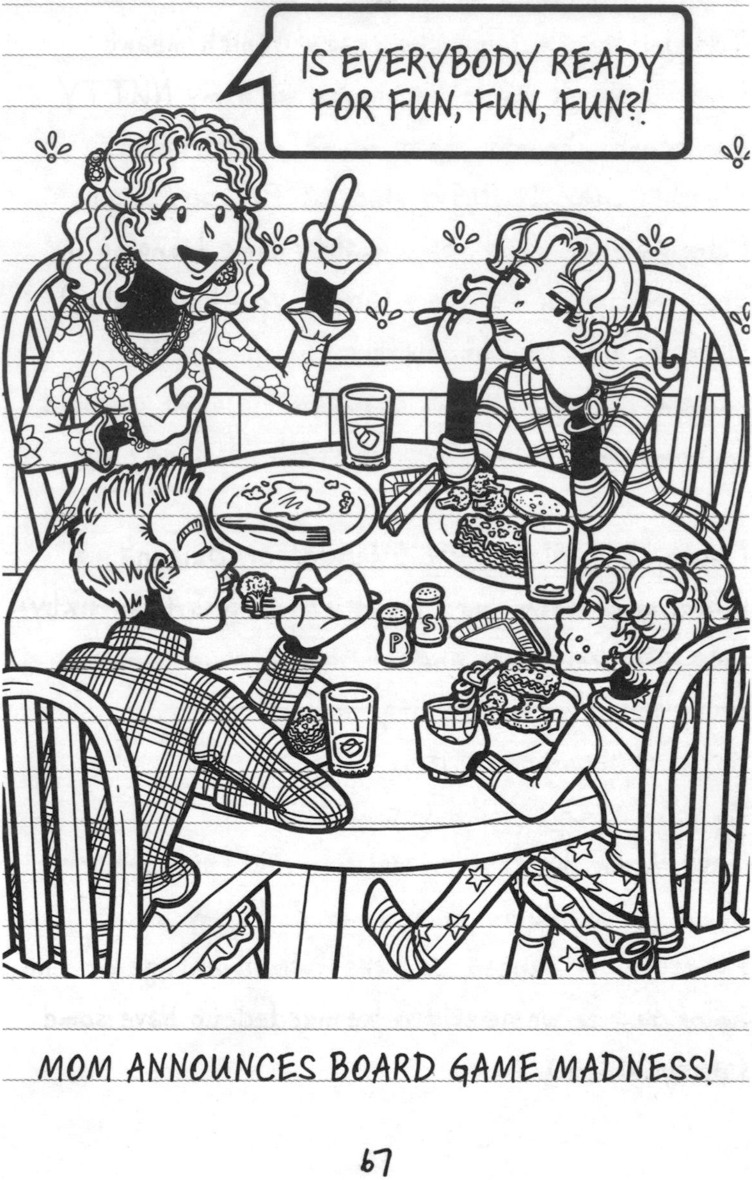
IS EVERYBODY READY FOR FUN, FUN, FUN?!
P
S

MOM ANNOUNCES BOARD GAME MADNESS!

I guess no one was ready for "FUN, FUN, FUN!" because the room was suddenly so quiet, you could hear the rainwater gurgling into the sewer drains outside.

On second thought, that sound was Brianna greedily GUZZLING a glass of Princess Sugar Plum punch.

"I really wish I could join the fun, dear!" Dad exclaimed. "But the big championship game is about to come on!"

"Same here, Mom! I'd LOVE to play an exciting board game with you!" I lied. "But my FAVE reality show, *My Very Rich and Trashy Life!*, will be on soon, and it's the thrilling finale!"

As soon as Dad and I got up from the table to leave, Mom shot us her evil sit-your-butts-back-down-if-you-know-what's-good-for-you look.

So of course we quickly returned to our chairs and sat down.

It's NEVER a good idea to tick off Mom.

As the wise old saying goes, "If Mom's NOT happy, then NOBODY'S happy!"

Which is actually just the trendier "mommy power" version of the wise old saying "Misery LOVES company!"

"YAY! It's Board Game Madness!" Brianna cheered. "I'll go get a really FUN board game! Be right back!"

Mom escorted Dad and me into the family room like a seasoned prison guard.

I almost expected her to handcuff us to the couch to prevent us from attempting a dangerous felonious act like turning on the TV.

About five minutes later Brianna came skipping into the room with a small bag behind her back and an old pizza box covered in finger paint and glitter.

"Look at this! I made my OWN game! It's called Brianna's Funnest Game Ever! You're gonna LOVE it! Can we play it?! Can we, Mom? PLEEEEASE?" Brianna pleaded. . . .

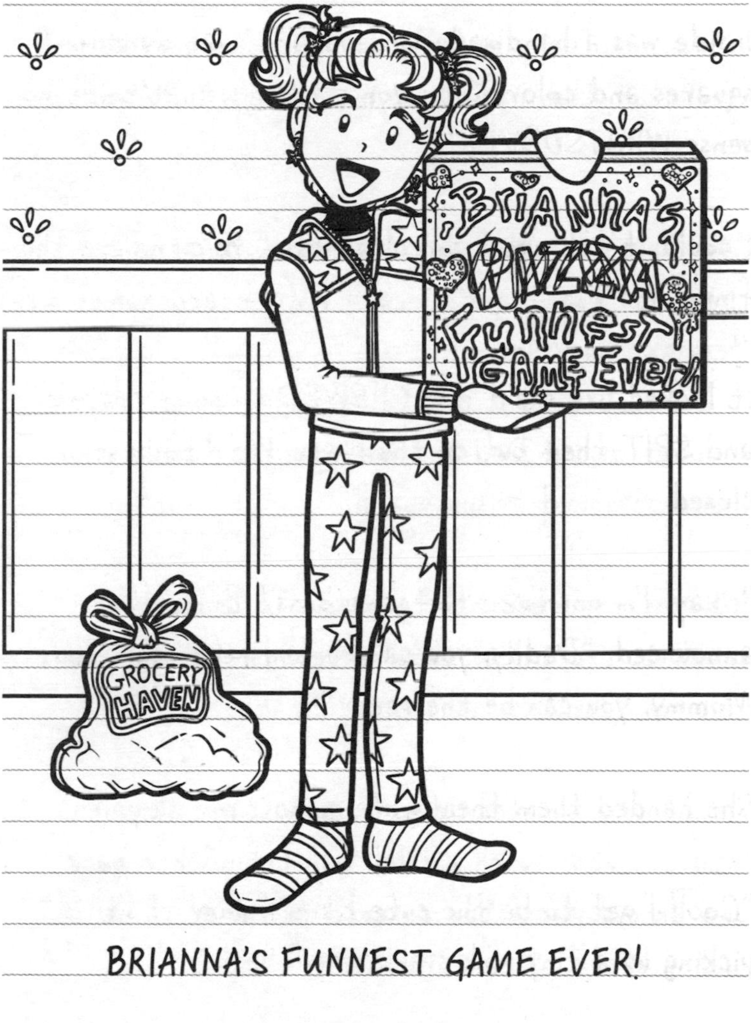
BRIANNA'S PIZZA Funnest GAME Ever!
GROCERY HAVEN

BRIANNA'S FUNNEST GAME EVER!

"We'd LOVE to play your game, sweetheart!" Mom smiled. "It's going to be FUN!"

Brianna opened her pizza box.

Inside was a handmade game board with random squares and colorful crayon scribbles that made no sense WHATSOEVER!

I couldn't tell which direction to move or where the finish line was.

It looked like she'd just CHEWED up some crayons and SPIT them out on the paper. With her eyes closed.

"Okay! I'm gonna be the game boss," Brianna announced. "Daddy, you can be the paper clip, and Mommy, you can be the penny."

She handed them their game pieces.

"Cool! I get to be the cute Barbie shoe!" I smiled, picking up a tiny pink sparkly high heel.

"NUH–UH!" Brianna grunted, and snatched it right out of my hand. "That's MINE! Remember, it's MY game! I made it, so I'M the BOSS of it!"

Then she stuck her tongue out at me.

I folded my arms and glared at her.

"Then what am I supposed to use to play your game?! There's nothing left!" I grumbled.

Brianna checked inside the box, and sure enough, there WEREN'T any more game pieces.

But she just SHRUGGED her shoulders at me like it WASN'T her problem!

That's when I got a BRILLIANT idea! . . .

"OH NO! It looks like I won't be able play your game, Brianna! I'm SO disappointed!" I pretend-pouted, like I was about to cry. "I guess I'll just have to go watch the finale of My Very Rich and Trashy

Life! while you guys have all the FUN! But I'll get over it! BYE!"

"Hey! Wait a minute!" Brianna grinned as she peeled off a moldy piece of pepperoni that was stuck to the bottom of the box. "Here, Nikki! THIS is YOUR game piece!" . . .

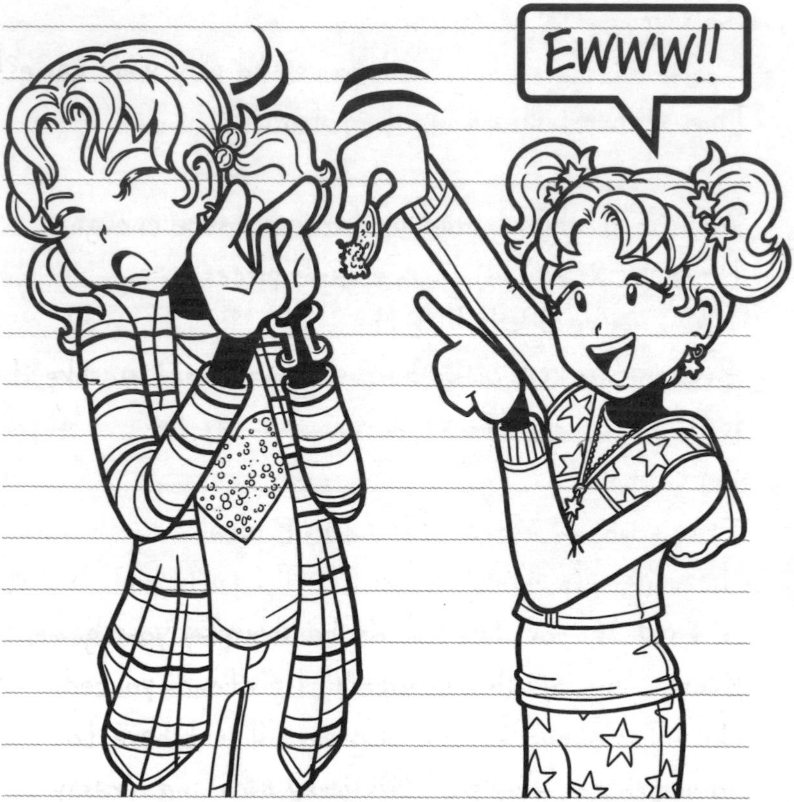
EWWW!!

"I don't want that nasty thing!" I shrieked.

"But it's the BEST one!" Brianna exclaimed. "If you get hungry and want a snack, you can chew on it! Then, when it's your turn to move again, you just put the pepperoni back on the game board. I bet you can chew it for hours! Just like gum."

That's when I threw up in my mouth a little.

"MOM?!" I whined, waiting for her to intervene.

"Nikki, you're SPOILING the fun!" Mom lectured. "Brianna worked really hard on this game, so simmer down! Just take the pepperoni and try to be a good sport, okay?"

I begrudgingly picked up my NASTY pepperoni, trying to avoid the fuzzy mold, and dropped it on the "start" box, which was misspelled "stat."

"Mommy, you go first," Brianna said.

Mom rolled the die and moved four spaces.

"Now, this is the fun part!" Brianna squealed, and pulled out a stack of index cards written in black marker in her sloppy handwriting. "You have to do whatever the card says!"

However, instead of taking a card from the top of the stack, Brianna quickly sorted through them until she found one she liked.

"Here, Mommy. This is YOUR card!"

Mom read the card. . . .

> YOU ARE NICE AND PRETTY
> LIKE PRINCESS SUGAR PLUM.
> MOVE FORWARD ~~SEVN~~ SEVEN
> SPACES!

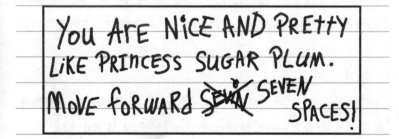

"How sweet!" Mom smiled and moved her penny seven spaces. "This game is FUN!"

"Okay, Daddy. Your turn!" Brianna chirped.

Dad rolled the die and moved five spaces.

Then Brianna selected a card. Dad read . . .

TodAY is YouR ~~LuckY~~ Lucky DAy!
Do THE "HOKEY PoKEY" AND THEN
MOVE AHEAD SIX SPACES!

"Woo-hoo!" Dad exclaimed. He hopped to his feet and did a rendition of the "Hokey Pokey" that included the chicken dance and some moves he stole from a Justin Bieber video.

Ugh!

Now I'll never be able to enjoy that video again without thinking of Dad's "Hokey Pokey"!

Next it was MY turn.

I tossed the die and moved three spaces.

"UH-OH!" Brianna said, reading the card she had selected for me.

She handed it to me, and I read it out loud. . . .

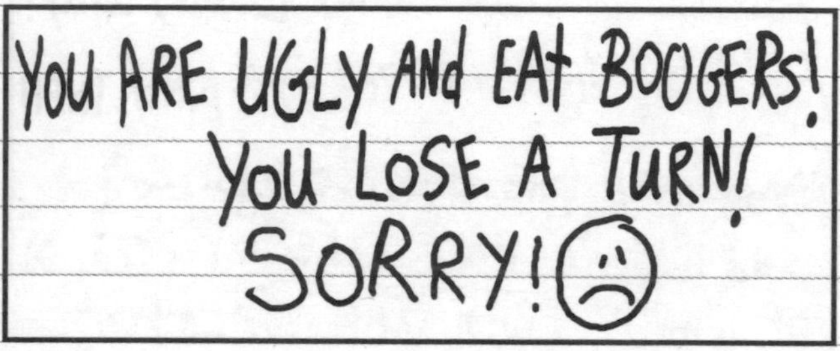
YOU ARE UGLY AND EAT BOOGERS!
YOU LOSE A TURN!
SORRY!

"WHAT?!" I shouted. "That's NOT FAIR! Why do I have to be the ugly, booger-eating . . . LOSER?!"

"Because it's *MY* game and *I* make the RULES!" Brianna said, all snotty-like, with her hand on her hip.

"Okay, FINE!" I grumped. "I thought this was supposed to be FUN!"

I was SO over Brianna's STUPID game!

"Hey, everyone, NOW it's MY turn!" Brianna giggled. She rolled the die and moved her Barbie shoe three spaces.

"Now I get a card!" she said as she quickly sorted through the stack until she found one she liked.

"OH, GOODY! My card says . . ."

> YOU ARE THE BESTEST PLAYER AND GET TO HAVE THREE PIECES OF OF CANDY FROM THE JACKPOT CANDY STASH! CONGRATULATIONS!!!

"WHAT jackpot candy stash?!" I exclaimed.

"THIS ONE!" Brianna answered as she grabbed the plastic bag and opened it.

I almost had a . . .

HEART ATTACK!

Inside was my PRECIOUS candy stash!!!

THAT BRATTY LITTLE THIEF HAD SNUCK INTO MY ROOM AND STOLEN MY ENTIRE STASH OF CANDY?!!

"NO WAY!!" I protested. "I HATE this CRUDDY game. GIMME BACK MY CANDY, BRIANNA!"

"Aw, come on, Nikki! It's just candy. You can always get more!" Dad scolded me. "Let's just try to have fun playing your little sister's game!"

"I agree! This is an opportunity for you to be an excellent role model for Brianna. So try not to be a SORE LOSER!" Mom admonished me.

It's no wonder I had a really bad attitude about the whole thing.

Every time it was MY turn, I ended up with a stupid card that said something like . . .

YoU GoTS COOTiES WiThOUT A COOTiE SHOt! Go tO JAiL! SORRY!!! ☹

Or . . .

YoU STiNkS REALly BAd ANd ~~NEd~~ NEED A BAth! GO BACk tO ~~STAt~~ StArt. ANd thEN LOSE A TURN!! SORRY!!!! ☹

And whenever it was Brianna's turn, she got to eat several more pieces of MY candy. I sat there GLARING at the three of them in complete DISGUST! I couldn't believe I was being FORCED by my very OWN parents to watch my bratty sister DEVOUR my candy during the finale of *My Very Rich and Trashy Life!*

I was very tempted to call the authorities and report them for CHILD ABUSE ☹!!

80

Finally Brianna had made an ingenious plan to get her GRUBBY little hands on my PROPERTY!

By the end of the game, my sister had eaten almost half of my candy! She had chocolate all over her face and hands and was looking a little queasy. . . .

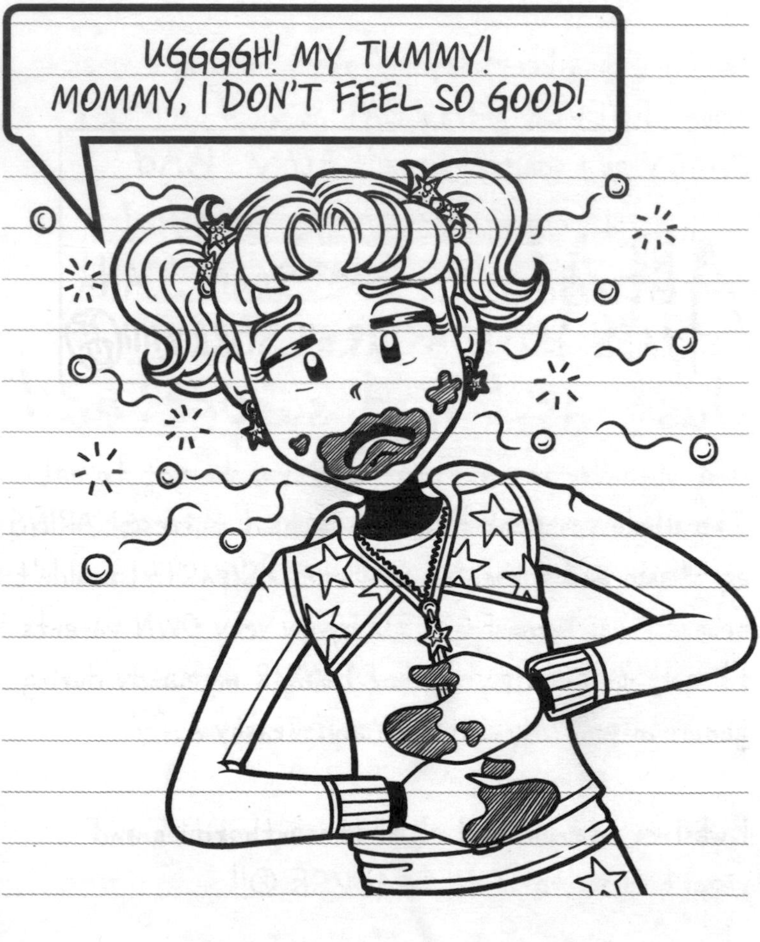
UGGGGH! MY TUMMY! MOMMY, I DON'T FEEL SO GOOD!

"Goodness! I think this game has gotten completely out of hand!" Mom said, looking a bit flustered.

Dad scooped Brianna up off the floor. "You've had way too many sweets, young lady. I think you need to get some rest to cure that tummy ache."

"But I wanna keep playing!" she whined in a weak voice. "I NEVER get to EAT as much of Nikki's CANDY as I want!"

AHA!
Just as I had suspected!!

The whole point of Brianna's game was to get into my stash, and Mom and Dad had fallen for it.

I'll give Brianna points for being a pigtailed evil genius in pink My Little Pony sneakers!

But I refuse to feel all that sorry for her.

The next time we have Board Game Madness, we're going to play a RIGGED game MY way!

My board game will be called BROCCOLI-OPOLY, and it'll feature ALL the foods that Brianna HATES!!

Watch your back, little sister!

You're going to get a big green nasty PAYBACK! And it's going to be HEALTHY!

I can't wait to give Brianna a special card that says . . .

Today is your lucky day! You get to drink a gallon of green smoothie! Sorry! ☹

And who knows! If I'm feeling really VENGEFUL, I just might toss in some MOLDY PEPPERONI for extra flavor!

Anyway, since *My Very Rich and Trashy Life!* is over, I might as well try to finish the homework I've been procrastinating all weekend.

I'm actually looking forward to school tomorrow.

I'll finally get to meet the NHH exchange student, Andrea.

It's going to be FUN!

SQUEEEEEE!!

☺!!

MONDAY, MAY 26—12:15 P.M.
IN THE GIRLS' BATHROOM

I was supposed to hang out with Chloe, Zoey, and Brandon during lunch to help them with their projects.

Chloe and Zoey want to start shooting practice videos next week.

And Brandon needs to get the Fuzzy Friends donation page up and running before their annual charity drive, which starts on June 5.

But, unfortunately, I had to cancel because I have an earlier lunch and I had to meet the exchange student at noon. And since this student ambassador thing is MANDATORY, I didn't have a choice.

At noon I grabbed my welcome sign and rushed down to the office.

I waited right outside the door. . . .

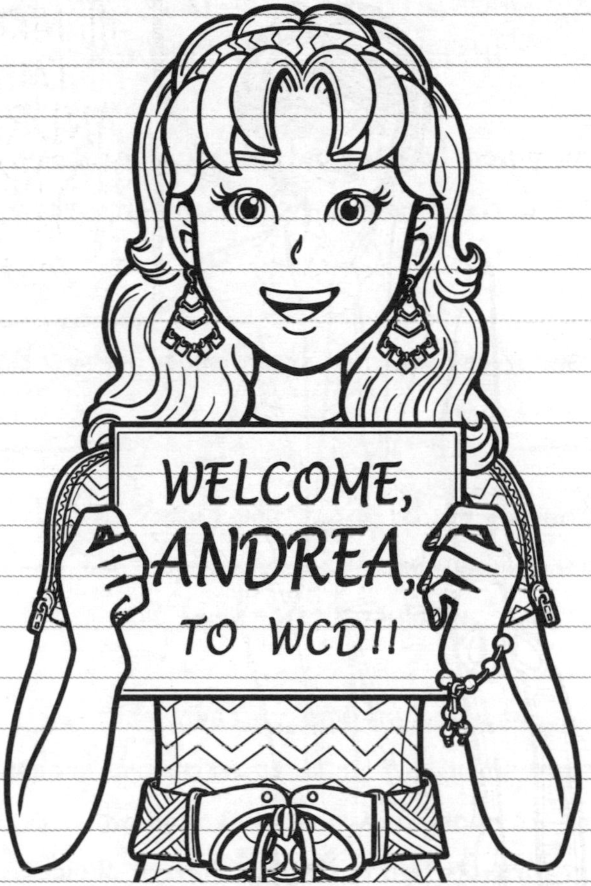
WELCOME, ANDREA, TO WCD!!

But soon it became very clear that I'd made a HUGE mistake. HOW could I have accidentally gotten something as simple as a NAME wrong?!

The exchange student's name WASN'T Andrea! . . .

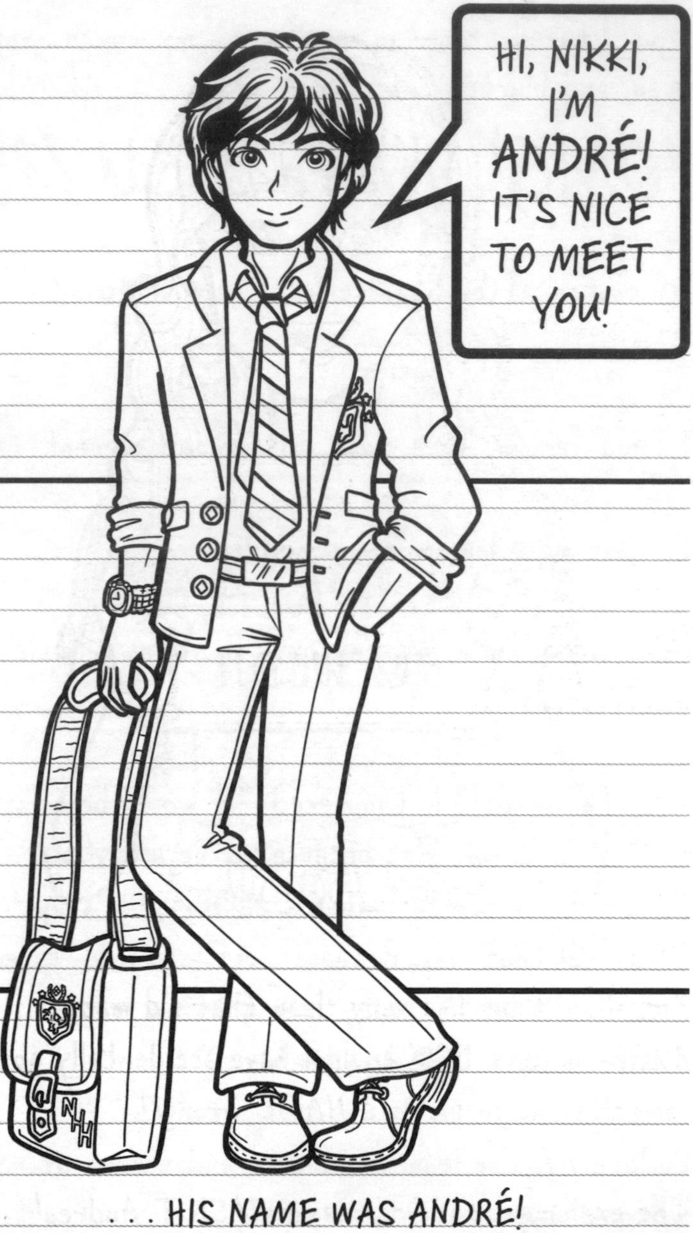
HI, NIKKI, I'M ANDRÉ! IT'S NICE TO MEET YOU!
NHH

. . . HIS NAME WAS ANDRÉ!

I just stared at him in shock, with my mouth hanging open, and blurted out . . .

"OMG! You're a GUY?!"

Of course, after I said that, I felt REALLY STUPID.

I could feel my face flush with embarrassment.

He gave me a big smile and nodded.

"Yes, Nikki. I'm a guy. I'm sorry if you're a little disappointed."

"NO! I'm n—not!" I stammered. "It would be STUPID to feel that way just because you're a guy! Uh, I mean . . . for ME. I'm NOT calling YOU stupid if YOU feel that way. Because most guys are—I mean, AREN'T! What I'm really trying to say is, um, is it ME or is it really WARM in here?"

Suddenly André leaned in closer and stared at my welcome sign. . . .

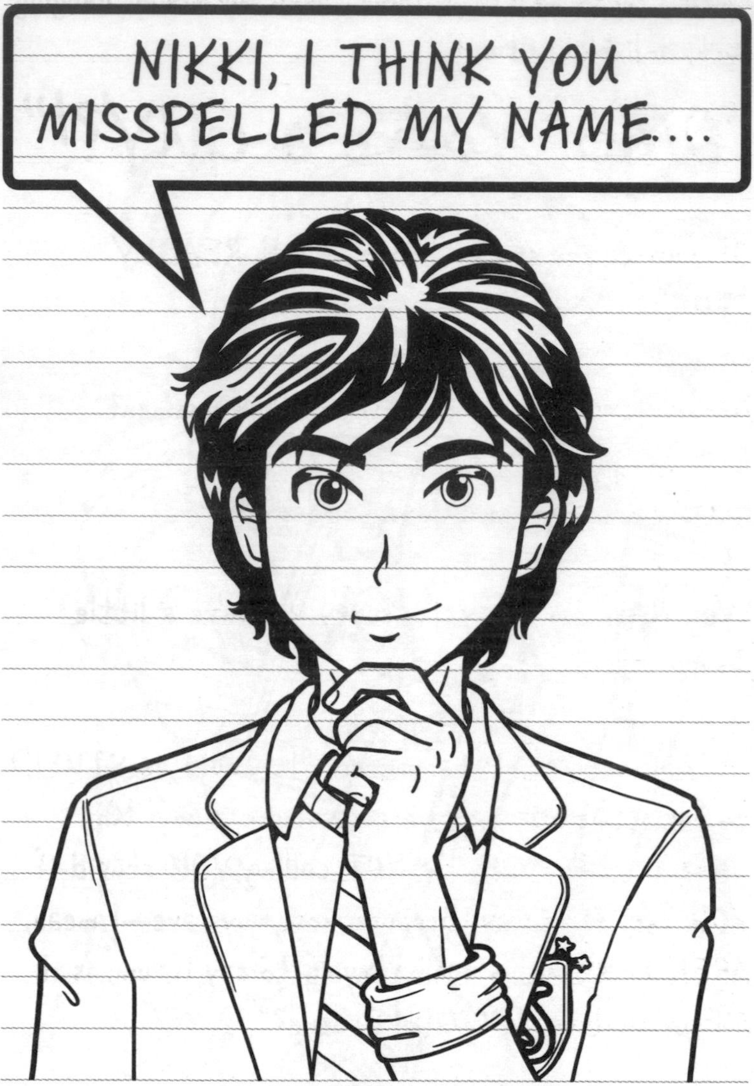
NIKKI, I THINK YOU MISSPELLED MY NAME....

ANDRÉ NOTICES MY SIGN.

I tried to cover up the misspelled name and act like it wasn't a big deal. . . .

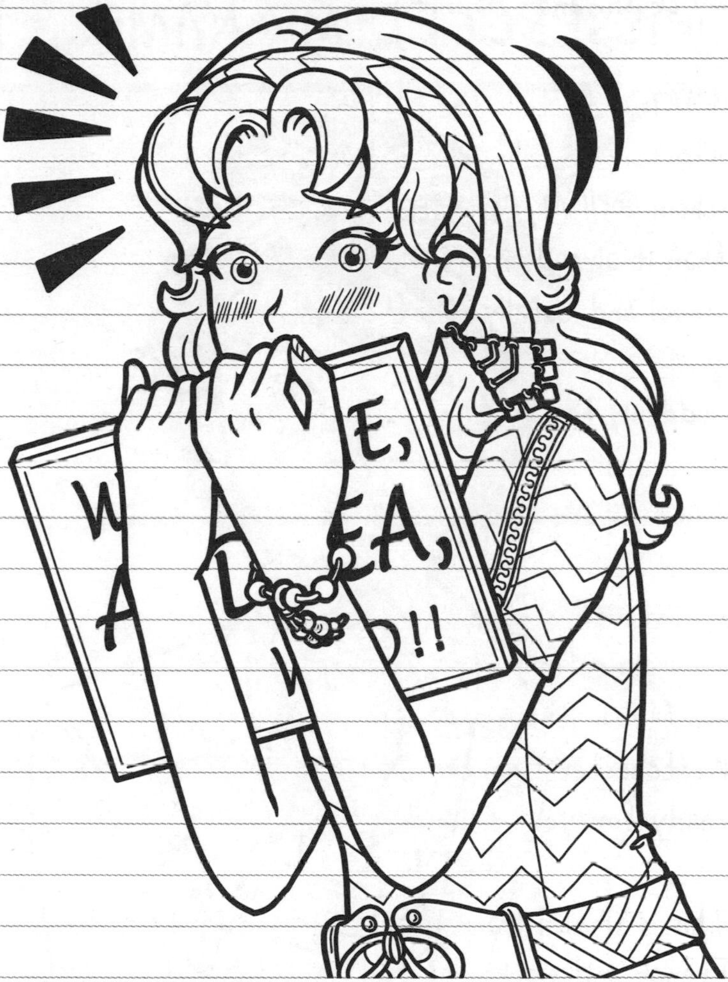

But inside I was totally FREAKING OUT!

OMG! I could NOT believe I had told a GUY all that VERY personal stuff about my hairy legs, my crush, and "Branikki."

WHAT if he tells the ENTIRE school ☹?! Worse yet, WHAT if he tells MY entire school and HIS entire school ☹?!! My reputation would be more PATHETIC than it already is. The gossip could follow me into high school and totally ruin the best years of my life.

Suddenly I realized that André was staring at me.

"Um . . . are you okay?" he asked.

I plastered a fake smile across my face and very cheerfully said, "André, it's nice to finally meet you. I hope you enjoy your week here at Westchester Country Day Middle School. Are you ready for your tour?"

This is what I learned about him. André's dad is French and works for the United Nations, and his mom is an American journalist. His mom and stepdad live here, and his dad has a home both here and in

Paris. He said he studied at the Louvre museum's program for gifted students and would LOVE to show me around the city if I ever visited Paris.

Then the WEIRDEST thing happened. André kind of stared at me and asked if he could call me Nicole instead of Nikki. He said the name Nicole is popular in France and is a beautiful and intriguing name, meaning "victorious," that fits me so much better.

OMG! I almost DIED from the massive drop in blood pressure due to intense blushing.

"Um . . . sure, André! Actually, my real name IS Nicole," I gushed, and then giggled.

André seems almost . . . PERFECT! Like, straight out of one of Chloe's teen romance books perfect!

I don't know what's WRONG with me. When he asked me what my favorite subject is, I completely blanked.

I also couldn't remember my locker combo.

I was looking for my phone to type in his cell number when I had it in my hand.

That's when I very politely asked André to wait in the library (I found the library ONLY because we were standing right in front of it) while I went to the girls' bathroom across the hall to check to see if I had left my BRAIN in there!

Yes! I just said my **BRAIN!** Or maybe I accidentally flushed it down the toilet when I was in there earlier today. Because right now I'm CLEARLY functioning WITHOUT ONE ☹!!

So I rushed to the girls' bathroom to try to pull myself together, because I was having a MASSIVE MELTDOWN! I gave myself a pep talk: Just stay calm. YOU can do this. Breathe deeply and repeat . . .

"I CAN DO THIS! I CAN DO THIS! I CAN DO THIS! I CAN DO THIS!"

Great job! Now just look at yourself in the mirror and say it one last time. . . .

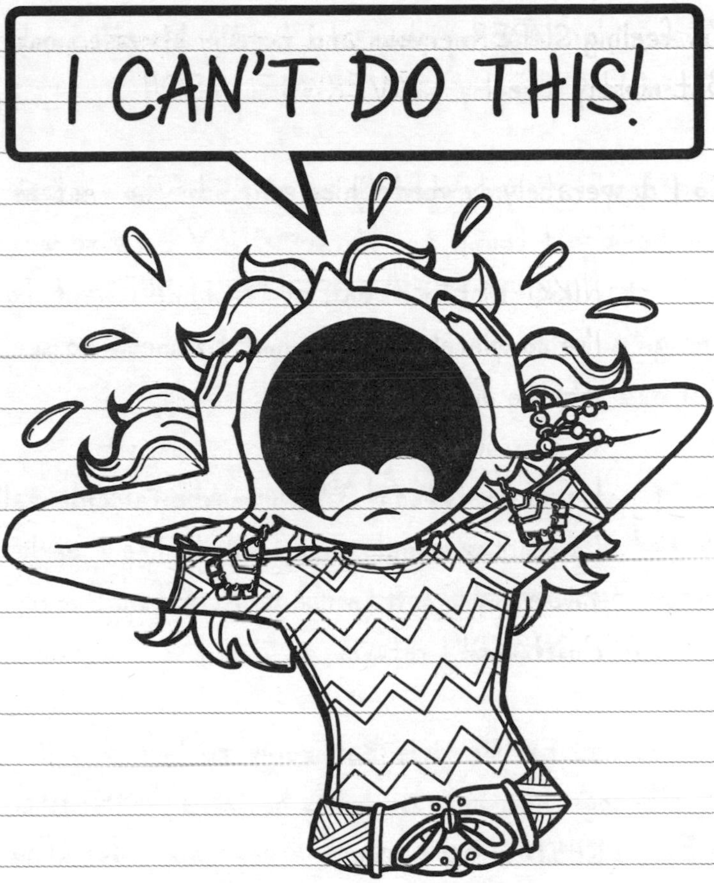
I CAN'T DO THIS!

ME, HAVING A MASSIVE MELTDOWN!!

To make matters WORSE, I just got a really important e-mail.

But I'm afraid to open and read it.

I'm feeling SUPERnervous and totally stressed out!
But mostly I feel . . . OVERWHELMED!!

So I desperately texted Chloe and Zoey a message:

NIKKI: HEEEEEEEEEEEEELP ☹!!
I've completely lost my mind! And since
it's the only one I have, I'm leaving
to go search for it. But if my mind
happens to wander back here before
I find it, please do me a really big
favor and lock it in the janitor's
closet until I return.

ZOEY: ??????????

CHLOE: R U insane?!!!!!

NIKKI: Probably. Just left a
ridiculously cute guy in the library
and rushed to the bathroom to
SCREAM at myself in the mirror!
Be right back! Checking toilet for
my missing brain.

CHLOE: ????????

ZOEY: ????????

NOTE TO SELF!!

Do not open the e-mail you just received from
Madame Danielle, the French teacher from NHH,
with the subject line "RE: DECISION REGARDING
ARTS & CULTURE STUDENT TRIP TO PARIS."

WHY?

Because if I have to deal with any more DRAMA,
my HEAD is going to EXPLODE!!

And I do NOT want to be publicly HUMILIATED
when my head EXPLODES at school in front of
the entire student body.

And, um . . . André.

☹!!

I've spent almost two hours giving André a complete tour of WCD.

Unlike some NHH students, he seems pretty friendly and has a wicked sense of humor.

We got along really well, and get this! WE BOTH LOVE ART!

The only problem is that he makes me SUPERnervous!

I don't know why. He just . . . DOES!!

André hasn't had a chance to meet any other students yet.

Although, after my crazy text messages, Chloe and Zoey are DYING to meet HIM.

In just the past hour my BFFs have texted me more than a dozen times.

97

My phone was chiming so much I turned off the sound.

I couldn't believe they were actually begging me to take a selfie with André and SEND it to them so they could "see what a HUNK he is!"

Sorry, Chloe and Zoey ☹! But I've only known the guy for, like, five minutes.

I am NOT going to embarrass myself by saying, "Um, André, would you mind taking a quick selfie with me? My BFFs are just DYING to see how HUNKY you are!"

Like, how JUVENILE would that be?!

At least Chloe and Zoey weren't too upset with me earlier when I told them I couldn't meet them today to work on their video project.

After André and I completed the tour, I showed him his locker and told him to text me if he had questions about anything.

He had to leave school early for a dentist appointment, so I walked him to the main entrance.

I thought his dad was waiting to pick him up at the front of the school, but he said it was his chauffeur! . . .

Yes! The guy is in middle school and has his own CHAUFFEUR!

Can you believe it?!

Must be **NICE!!**

We agreed to meet tomorrow morning at my locker and then head off to class.

After André left, I decided to go ahead and read that e-mail about the Paris trip in August. I wasn't supposed to find out if I'd been accepted for another week still, but I was pretty sure this was a big fat REJECTION!

Even if my head exploded, the only person around was MacKenzie, and she couldn't care less.

Unless, of course, a teeny tiny bit splattered on her shoe. In which case, she'd have a complete meltdown!

I held my breath as I nervously read the e-mail: "Dear Nikki, Blah, blah, blah-blah, blah-blah . . ."

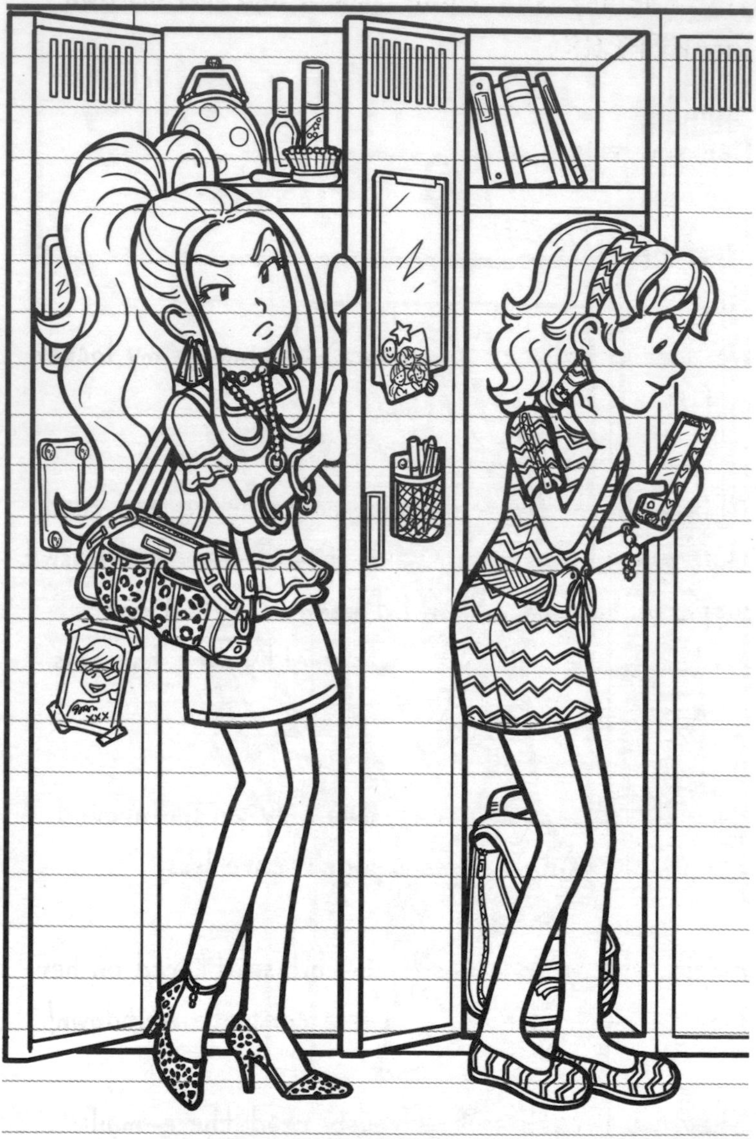

ME, NERVOUSLY READING THE E-MAIL

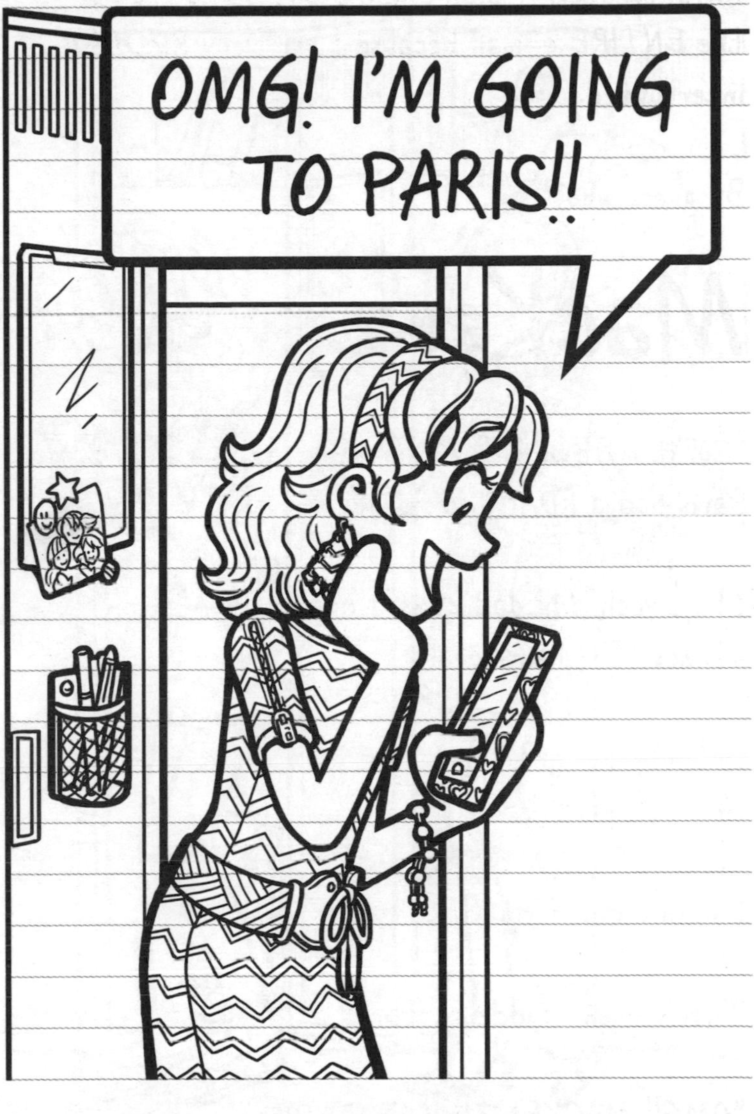
OMG! I'M GOING TO PARIS!!

I ACTUALLY GOT A SPOT ON THE TRIP!!

Unfortunately, I didn't get a chance to read the ENTIRE e-mail because I was very RUDELY interrupted.

By guess who?! . . .

MacKenzie ☹!!

"So, it must be a family business trip? I didn't know Paris had a ROACH problem!" she giggled.

Okay, yeah. My dad owns a bug extermination business. Big hairy deal!

But why did girlfriend have to start tossing NASTY insults?

I wasn't even TALKING to her ☹!

That's when I suddenly stared at MacKenzie in horror.

"OMG!! MACKENZIE!! IT'S YOUR . . . NOSE!!" I gasped. "I can't believe it. Your NOSE!"

She immediately panicked and touched her nose.

"WHAT'S WRONG WITH MY NOSE?!"

"IT'S IN MY BUSINESS! AGAIN!" I exclaimed. "PLEASE! KEEP YOUR NOSE OUT OF MY BUSINESS!"

MacKenzie just rolled her eyes at me. "Nikki, instead of worrying about my nose, you should worry about your face. You're so BUTT UGLY that when dogs first meet you, they sniff your FACE! I know you're JEALOUS, Nikki, but don't HATE ME because I'm beautiful!"

"You actually think I'm jealous?! MacKenzie, you have FAKE hair, FAKE nails, FAKE eyelashes, and a FAKE tan! I can actually BUY your beauty SUPERcheap at the Dollar Store!"

"Well, don't feel TOO bad, Nikki! You can always PHOTOSHOP the photos of your face!"

"At least I have hope, MacKenzie. You can't Photoshop your BUTT-UGLY PERSONALITY! But your dad's really rich! So you can ask him to BUY you a new one for your birthday!"

That's when MacKenzie just totally ignored me.

She glanced in her mirror and slathered on, like, four layers of Pretty Peach sparkly lip gloss.

Then she flipped her hair, rolled her eyes at me one final time, and SASHAYED AWAY.

I just HATE it when MacKenzie SASHAYS!

MacKenzie is SOOO aggravating!

She makes me want to . . .

SCREAM!!

But instead of thinking about MacKenzie, I decided to concentrate on my FABULOUS summer plans!

They were EXCITING enough to make even MacKenzie GREEN with envy!

JUNE: Um . . . have I mentioned yet that my birthday is in June?

JULY: I'll be on tour with my BFFs in July.

AUGUST: I'll do Paris in August.

SEPTEMBER: And then high school in September!

I was NOT about to let MacKenzie's silly MEAN GIRL shenanigans RUIN my good mood!

Besides, I was too distracted. I was already envisioning myself taking selfies in PARIS! . . .

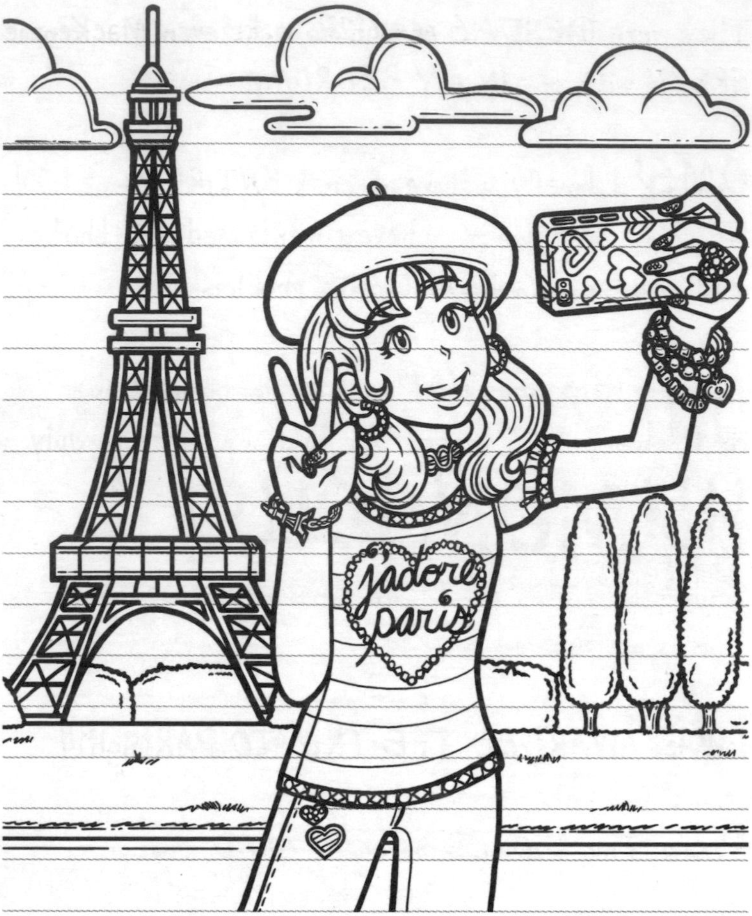
j'adore paris

ME IN PARIS

This is going to be the BEST summer of my ENTIRE life!! ☺!!

TUESDAY, MAY 27—6:45 A.M.
IN MY BEDROOM

OMG! I finally just read that ENTIRE e-mail ☹!

And now I have a REALLY big problem!

Actually, BIG does NOT even begin to describe it. It's . . .

HUMONGOUS!

This is my problem. . . .

I WAS AWARDED THE TRIP TO PARIS ☹!!

I know. This SHOULD be really GOOD news.

I should be doing my Snoopy "happy dance" on top of my bed, NOT lying here SUPERdepressed, staring at the wall and SULKING.

I reread the e-mail that I'd received from Madame Danielle for the FIFTH time. . . .

FROM: Madame Danielle

TO: Nikki Maxwell

RE: Decision Regarding Arts & Culture Student Trip to Paris

Dear Nikki,

Congratulations! You have been selected to participate in the Arts & Culture Student Trip to Paris, France, sponsored this year by North Hampton Hills International Academy.

You will be receiving your Paris Student Travel Registration Packet very soon. However, please be aware that the attached Parental Permission Form must be signed and returned by the deadline of Wednesday, June 11, to reserve your spot in the program.

We are happy to announce that we are expanding our program from ten to fourteen days. To accommodate this change, our trip will take place this year from July 7 to July 20. If you have any questions or concerns, please feel free to contact me.

Best regards,

Madame Danielle

I was hoping that I had somehow simply misread the dates of the trip.

But I hadn't!

My trip to Paris is scheduled for two weeks in July, right smack in the middle of my BAD BOYZ tour!

NOOOOOOO ☹!!

That was me SCREAMING.

I can't believe I'm going to have to choose between the two—PARIS or the CONCERT TOUR ☹! It's going to be almost IMPOSSIBLE to do!

The fourteen-day trip to Paris is a once-in-a-lifetime opportunity for me to study art at the world-famous Louvre.

However, the Bad Boyz tour will be an awesome experience for my friends and me! And I'm sure it would increase the popularity of our band.

I think I need to talk to Brandon, Chloe, and Zoey about this since it involves them.

But I'm pretty sure they'll probably just tell me to follow my heart.

I think they'll support whatever decision I make.

I'm so LUCKY to have friends like them!

OMG!

This is the most difficult decision I've ever had to make in my entire life.

!!

My day with André has been a complete CIRCUS!

When I introduced him to Chloe and Zoey this morning, they pretty much lost their minds.

"André, these are my BFFs, Chloe Garcia and Zoey Franklin," I said.

"Hi, Chloe and Zoey, it's nice to meet you!" André said as he shook their hands. "Any BFF of Nicole's is a BFF of mine!"

"Hi, André!" Chloe said, batting her eyes really fast like her contacts had completely dried out or something.

"Nice to meet you, André!" Zoey practically whispered, and then giggled uncontrollably.

I didn't know what had gotten into my friends. WHY were they acting so silly?!

"So, André, are you ready to head off to our first class?" I asked.

"I'll come too, if you don't mind," Chloe giggled.

"Me too!" Zoey squealed.

That's when I noticed that a small crowd of girls, including MacKenzie, had gathered. They were giggling and staring at André.

MacKenzie gave André a big smile and waved. "Hi, I'm MacKenzie Hollister! Welcome to WCD. If you need anything at all, including a SMART, cute, and fashionable friend to hang out with, just let ME know!"

Well, at least she was right about the cute and fashionable part.

I could not believe it when she started twirling her hair around and around, trying to secretly hypnotize him into doing her EVIL bidding (she had tried that same stunt with Brandon!). . . .

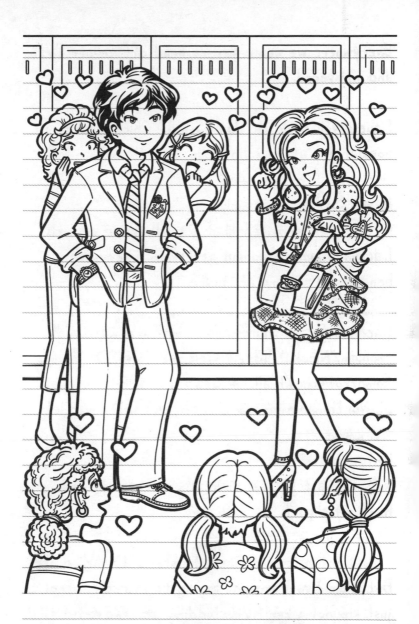

MACKENZIE, FLIRTING WITH ANDRÉ

Everywhere we went, girls stopped, stared, giggled, and whispered.

I guess you could say that André was a VERY popular guy at my school.

It was SO embarrassing!

I actually apologized for some of their more juvenile behavior.

But André just smiled and shrugged it off. "No problem, Nicole. Today I'm the new kid. But by tomorrow they'll all be IGNORING me like they do at North Hampton Hills," he joked.

Unfortunately, things got a little tense in bio.

In all my classes, the teachers had allowed André to sit next to me since he was a visiting student.

But when Brandon saw André sitting in HIS seat, he just kind of stood there staring at him with this look that I'd never seen before. . . .

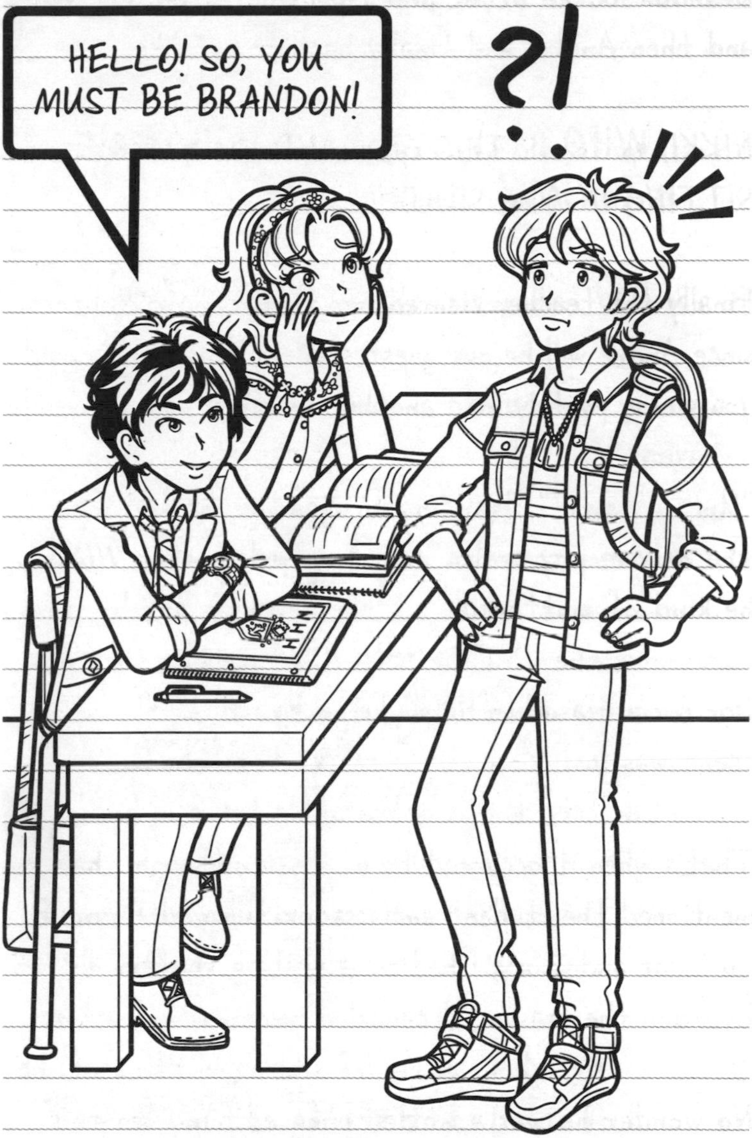
HELLO! SO, YOU MUST BE BRANDON!
?!

BRANDON MEETS ANDRÉ.

Brandon looked at me and then André, back to me and then André, and finally back to me, like . . .

NIKKI, **WHO** IS THIS GUY AND **WHY** IS HE SITTING IN **MY** SEAT?!!

Finally the teacher cleared her throat. "Mr. Roberts, since André will be our guest student this week, could you please politely find another seat?"

"Um . . . sure!" Brandon shrugged as he slid into the only empty seat. "Hey, bro, welcome to WCD," he kind of muttered.

For some reason I felt bad for Brandon. The whole scene was just kind of . . . AWKWARD!!

That's when it occurred to me that although I had mentioned the student ambassador thing with André to Chloe and Zoey, I had completely forgotten to tell Brandon the reason I'd canceled meeting him earlier.

No wonder he was a little confused. And very highly ANNOYED. . . .

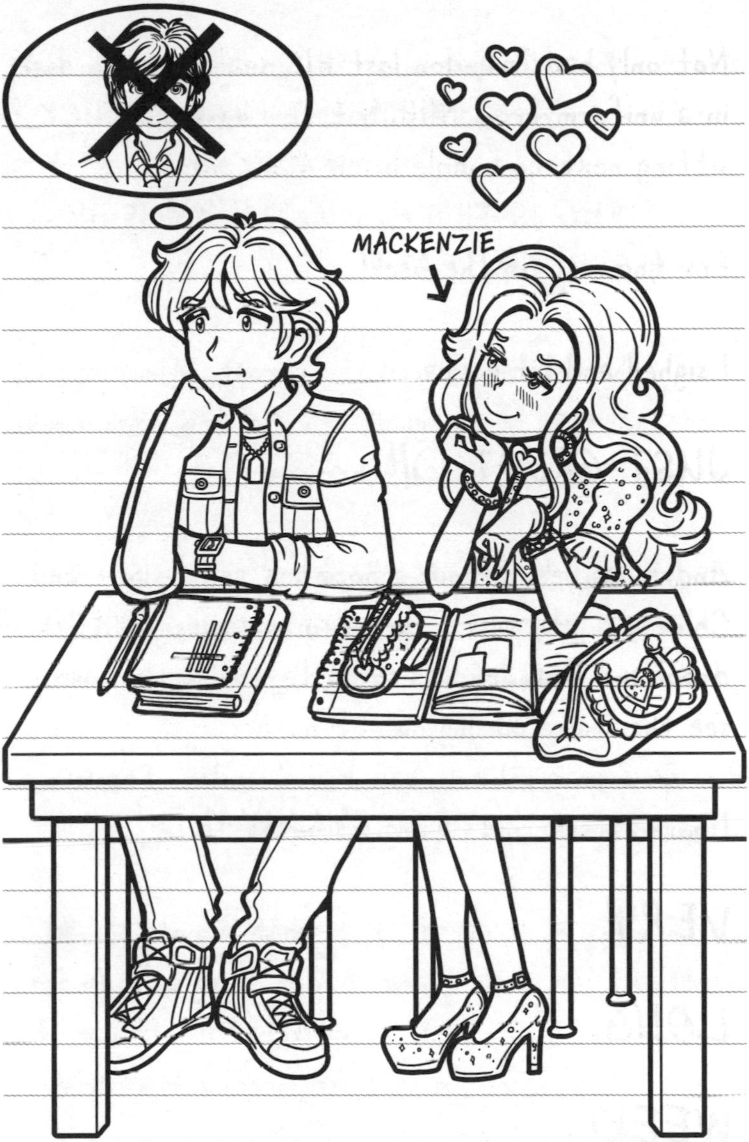
MACKENZIE

BRANDON, KIND OF TICKED OFF ABOUT THE NEW SEATING ARRANGEMENT!

Not only had Brandon lost HIS seat to some dude in a uniform from NHH, but now he was STUCK sitting next to bubble brain MacKenzie.

For the rest of the week!

I sighed and bit my lip.

JUST GREAT ☹!!

André has been at our school less than a day, and Chloe and Zoey have turned into giggling puddles of drool and Brandon was so irritated I could almost see the smoke coming out of his ears.

I have a feeling it's going to be a . . .

VERY.

LONG.

WEEK!

☹!!

WEDNESDAY, MAY 28—10:50 A.M.
AT MY LOCKER

André and I get along really well, and he's fitting right in at WCD.

Most of the students seem to really LOVE him!

And by "most students," I mean . . . GIRLS.

Some of the guys seem really bent out of shape with all the attention he's been getting.

"What's up with the dude in the cheesy school uniform?!" I overheard a few jocks complain yesterday when a dozen girls lined up to take selfies with André like he was a celeb or something.

Personally, I think those guys are a little jelly (a.k.a. jealous) of André.

At least Brandon is being a good sport about the whole thing.

He told me not to worry about trying to help out with the Fuzzy Friends website since I'm going to be SUPERbusy with my student ambassador duties.

Brandon is such a SWEETHEART ☺!

(Although he did text me this morning that he can hardly wait for André to go back to Hogwarts so he can get his seat back in bio.)

I just hope Brandon is able to get everything done in time for the annual fund-raiser since they need all the money they can get to keep the animal rescue center open.

Chloe and Zoey are my BFFs and I love them, but they've been acting so silly and immature around André that it's an EMBARRASSMENT!

The whole selfie FIASCO yesterday was actually THEIR fault. They practically BEGGED André for a selfie, and to be nice he agreed.

So the four of us took one together. . . .

ANDRÉ TAKES A SELFIE WITH
CHLOE, ZOEY, AND ME.

MacKenzie was at her locker the entire time,
pretending like my BFFs and I didn't EXIST.

So of course SHE asked André for a selfie too.

After that it was two girls from the drama club and then the ENTIRE cheerleading squad!

Pretty soon there were a dozen girls in line, all waiting to take a selfie with André.

But here's the really WEIRD part! . . .

EVERYONE kept telling me what a CUTE COUPLE André and I were.

I was like, "Um . . . NO WAY! We're actually just FRIENDS. We're only hanging out because I'm a student ambassador and it's MANDATORY."

But they just smiled like I was LYING to them and started WHISPERING to each other.

Of course I wondered what was going on!

So to avoid all the DRAMA that had occurred yesterday, I texted André and asked him to meet me in the library. I figured we'd hang out there for a while and then go straight to class.

I was surprised when he showed up with a bag from the CupCakery. . .

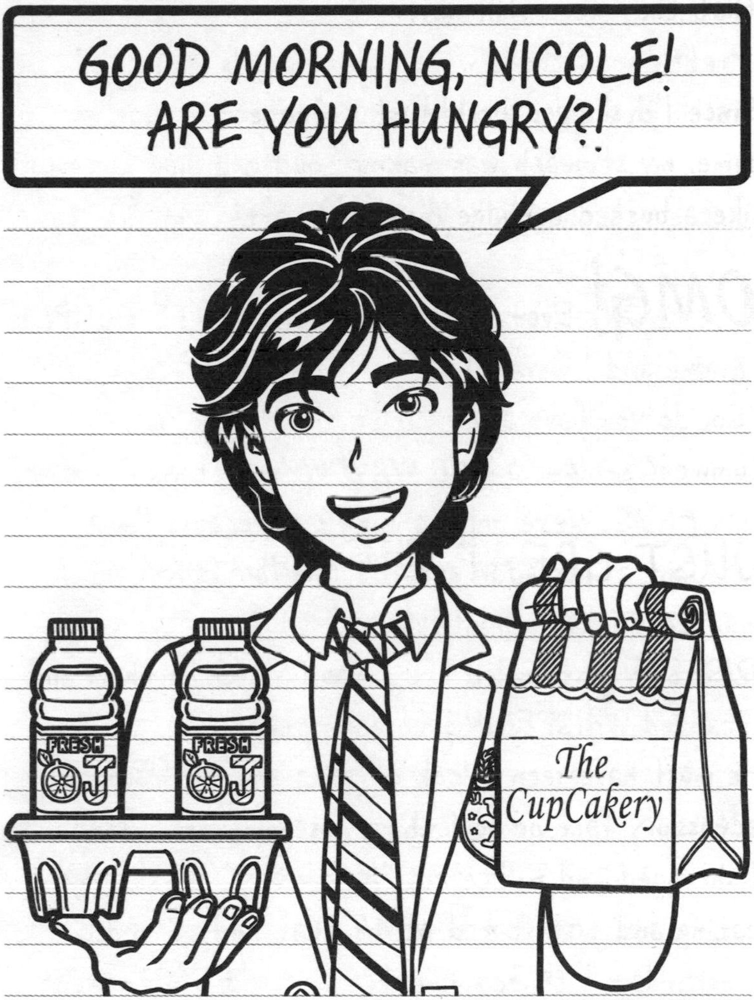
GOOD MORNING, NICOLE! ARE YOU HUNGRY?!
FRESH OJ
FRESH OJ
The CupCakery

ANDRÉ, BRINGING BREAKFAST

He'd purchased orange juice and extra-large cinnamon buns with cream cheese frosting. The best part was that they were still warm!

Since I'd skipped breakfast to get to school on time, my stomach was making loud grinding noises like a busted garbage disposal.

OMG! Everything was DELISH!

"So, do you have any exciting plans for the summer?" André asked.

JUST GREAT ☹!! The last thing I wanted to talk about was my summer scheduling DISASTER!

He must have seen a look of pure anguish flash across my face or something. Because even after I shrugged and muttered, "Not really," he stopped eating and just stared at me.

"Really?! Are your parents shipping you off to boot camp or something?" he teased.

Instead of answering, I just took a big bite of my cinnamon bun and chewed, trying not to look as annoyed as I felt. I'd already blabbed WAAAY too much about my PATHETIC life in those e-mails I'd sent André.

Hey, I barely even KNOW the guy!

"I WISH they were shipping me off to camp!" I finally sighed. "Then I wouldn't feel so guilty for being selfish and totally ruining my BFFs' plans for the summer!"

"Nicole, you don't seem to me like the type of person who'd purposely hurt your friends."

"Listen, André, it's REALLY complicated, and we don't have that much time," I muttered.

He glanced at his watch. "Actually, we have two minutes and fifteen seconds. I suggest you talk really, really fast!" He smiled.

So I reluctantly told him EVERYTHING! . . .

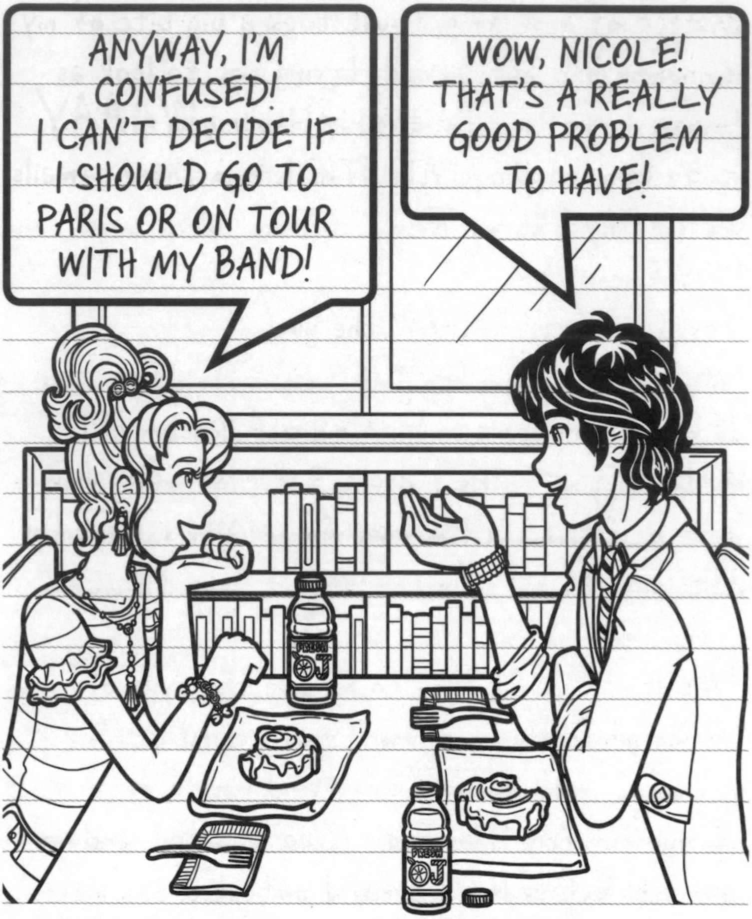
ANYWAY, I'M CONFUSED! I CAN'T DECIDE IF I SHOULD GO TO PARIS OR ON TOUR WITH MY BAND!
WOW, NICOLE! THAT'S A REALLY GOOD PROBLEM TO HAVE!

I SPILL MY GUTS TO ANDRÉ!

"Seriously, André! It's a BIG problem for ME if I disappoint my friends. I really care about them!" I explained.

"Wait a minute!" he exclaimed. "Let me get this straight. YOU have an all-expenses-paid trip for two weeks in Paris to study at the Louvre, and you're worried about your friends being MAD at you?! Really?! Sorry, Nicole, but you need some NEW friends!"

"Well, I don't know for SURE that they'd be mad at me. But I'd be mad at MYSELF. I'd basically be ditching my BFFs and the Bad Boyz tour that we've been planning together for MONTHS! Like, WHO does that?! Only the WORST friend EVER!" I grumbled.

"I'll be perfectly honest with you. I'd LOVE for you to come to Paris, Nicole! We'd have a great time hanging out together, and I could show you around the city. But that's a decision only YOU can make."

"OMG! Studying art in Paris would be a dream come true. Everyone was really HAPPY for me a few weeks ago when I first told them about it. I guess I need to sit down with them and explain that both events are scheduled at the same time. And if I go to Paris,

I WON'T be able to go with them on the Bad Boyz tour. I just hope they won't be too disappointed!"

Anyway, after hashing everything out with André, I decided to do the mature and responsible thing.

I sent Chloe, Zoey, and Brandon a text asking them to meet me after school in the library to discuss some really important news.

André said I shouldn't worry because everything was going to work out fine. I was so grateful for his help and advice that I told him I'd give him one of the Queasy Cheesy gift cards from my dad.

I just hope he's right!

☺!

WEDNESDAY—4:30 P.M.
AT HOME IN THE FAMILY ROOM

AAAAAAHHH ☹!!

Okay. THAT was me SCREAMING!!

WHY?

Because I am having yet another MELTDOWN!!

YES, I know! It's the SECOND one this week, and it's only Wednesday!

This is what happened. . . .

Chloe, Zoey, and Brandon were excited to meet me in the library after school.

André and I have been attending classes together for ONLY two DAYS, but my friends were acting more like it had been two WEEKS.

"Nikki, we know your student ambassador duties are mandatory, but we really miss hanging out with you!" Zoey complained.

"I totally agree!" Chloe grumbled. "André is a nice and cute guy, but it kind of feels like he has KIDNAPPED our BFF!"

"Yeah! Someone needs to tell that dude this place is a middle school, NOT a DAY CARE CENTER!" Brandon griped. "Personally, Nikki, I think he's into you."

"No way! It's NOT like that at all," I protested. "Come on, guys. Be NICE!"

But deep down I was surprised and very flattered that Brandon was acting a little jealous. Maybe it meant Brandon REALLY liked me.

Although, to be honest, it had never occurred to me that a guy like André would be interested in a nice and dorky girl like . . . ME!

I mean, he could totally date one of those gorgeous teen Disney starlets.

Hey, I'd be lucky to have ONE guy interested in me.

But TWO guys?!

OMG!

That sounds like something straight out of a fairy tale. . . .

Once upon a time, Princess Nikki was standing on her balcony gazing at her beautiful kingdom.

Suddenly the handsome Prince Brandon appeared and said, "Princess Nikki, would you like to go for a walk with ME in the meadow?"

But before she could answer, the handsome Prince André appeared and said, "Princess Nicole, would you like to walk with ME in the meadow?!"

Then they dueled over her with swords. . . .

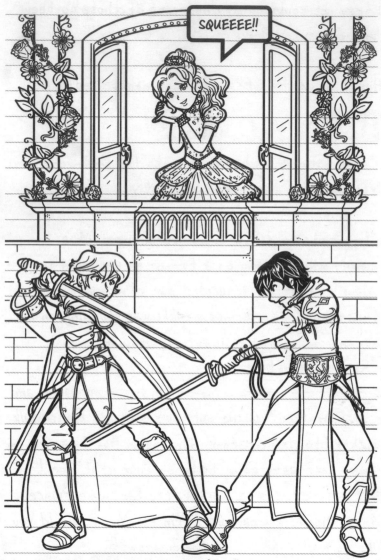

BRANDON AND ANDRÉ DUEL OVER ME
WITH SWORDS!

Zoey interrupted my daydream. "So, what's the important news? We're DYING to know!"

"Is it a SURPRISE?!" Chloe squealed. "I LOVE surprises!"

"Well, actually, it has to do with the Bad Boyz tour this summer," I answered hesitantly.

"I'm ready to ROCK!" Zoey exclaimed. "My family will be going on a two-week vacation to Maui without me. I decided our tour was more important!"

"Really?!" I muttered.

"Yeah, me too!" Chloe said. "I FINALLY landed us tickets to Comic-Con in San Diego. But I gave them away since we're going to be on tour that week!"

"You DID?!" I groaned.

"Same here!" Brandon said. "I've been on a waiting list for a photography camp, and I found out last

week that I got in! But I've already given up my spot since we'll be on tour in July."

"You DIDN'T!" I moaned.

All three of my friends stared at me eagerly as they waited for me to share my VERY important news.

Suddenly I felt really . . . GUILTY! Each of my friends had made a personal sacrifice to go on that tour.

"Well, actually, it's REALLY hard for me to find the right words," I muttered.

"Come on, Nikki! You can tell us ANYTHING!" Zoey said encouragingly.

I took a deep breath and closed my eyes.

"Okay! Chloe, Zoey, and Brandon, I realize we've been planning this Bad Boyz tour for MONTHS! But I really need to let you know that . . . I CAN'T—"

That's when my BFFs very enthusiastically and very rudely interrupted me. . . .

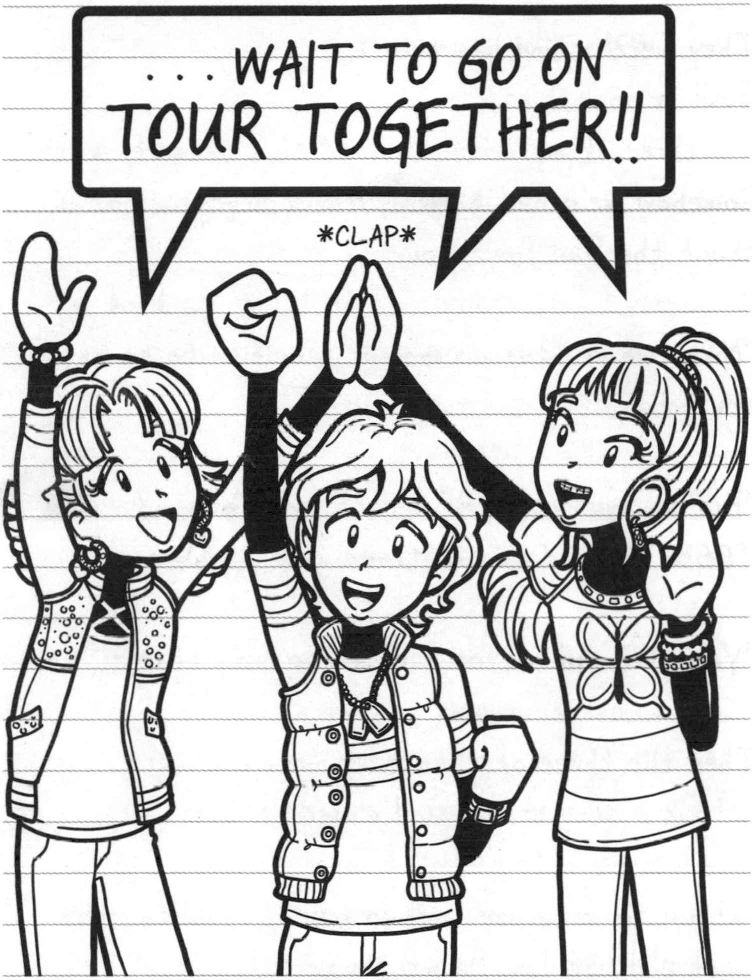
. . . WAIT TO GO ON TOUR TOGETHER!!
CLAP

MY SUPERENTHUSIASTIC BFFS

Then Chloe, Zoey, and Brandon started cheering! And WOO-HOOing! And high-fiving each other!

They were acting like they had just won the Super Bowl or something.

Somehow we'd had a MAJOR miscommunication about the Bad Boyz tour.

"Nikki, we realize our show is a huge responsibility for you," Zoey said supportively.

"But always remember! WE'RE in this thing TOGETHER!" Chloe said, giving me jazz hands.

"Yeah! WE GOT THIS!" Brandon exclaimed.

Then the three of them gave me a big hug!

The massive outpouring of love, support, and enthusiasm from my friends was SO touching that I got a HUGE lump in my throat.

I knew I was going to have to tell my friends the

TRUTH sooner or later. But right then I was kind of leaning more toward . . .

LATER ☹!

As much as I wanted to wait, though, I knew I had to get it over with. Since it seemed almost impossible for me to TELL them the bad news, I thought it might be easier if I just SHOWED them.

"Listen, guys, I want you to read an e-mail that I received on Monday. That will pretty much explain everything," I said.

I pulled up my e-mails to show them the one I'd gotten about the trip to Paris.

But that's when I noticed a brand-new e-mail from a popular social media website saying that a post I was tagged in had received more than twenty-five comments and likes.

It said "Cute pic of André and Nikki!" I opened the e-mail and just stared at the photo in shock. . . .

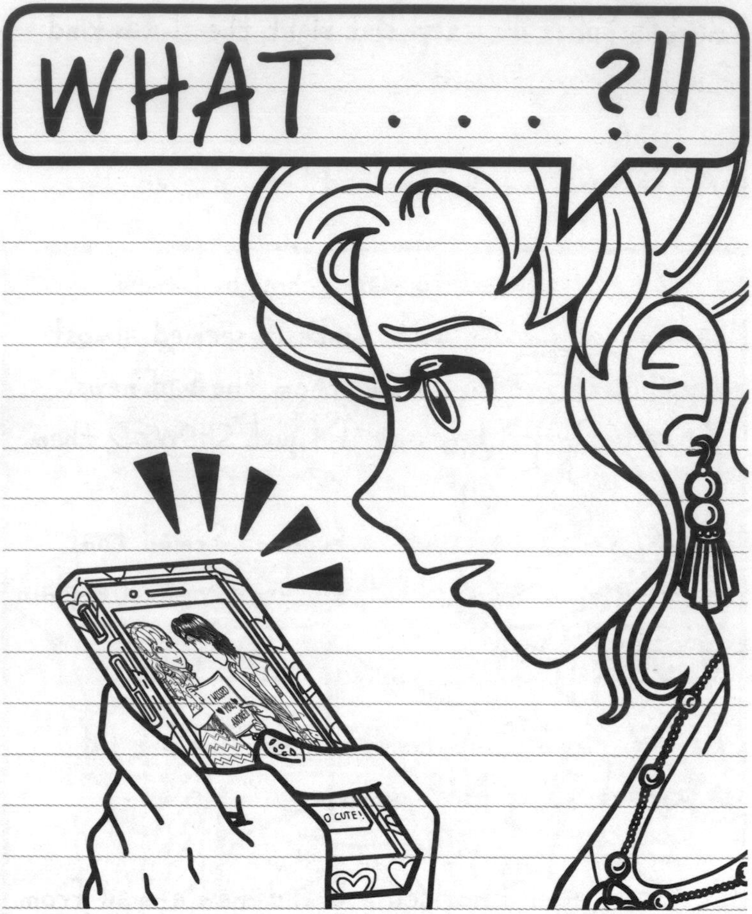
WHAT . . . ?!!

ME, FREAKING OUT OVER
A PIC OF ME ONLINE!

It FINALLY made sense why everyone was GOSSIPING yesterday about André and me being a couple.

Someone had taken a photo of André and me at school.

But the sign I was holding had been altered. . . .

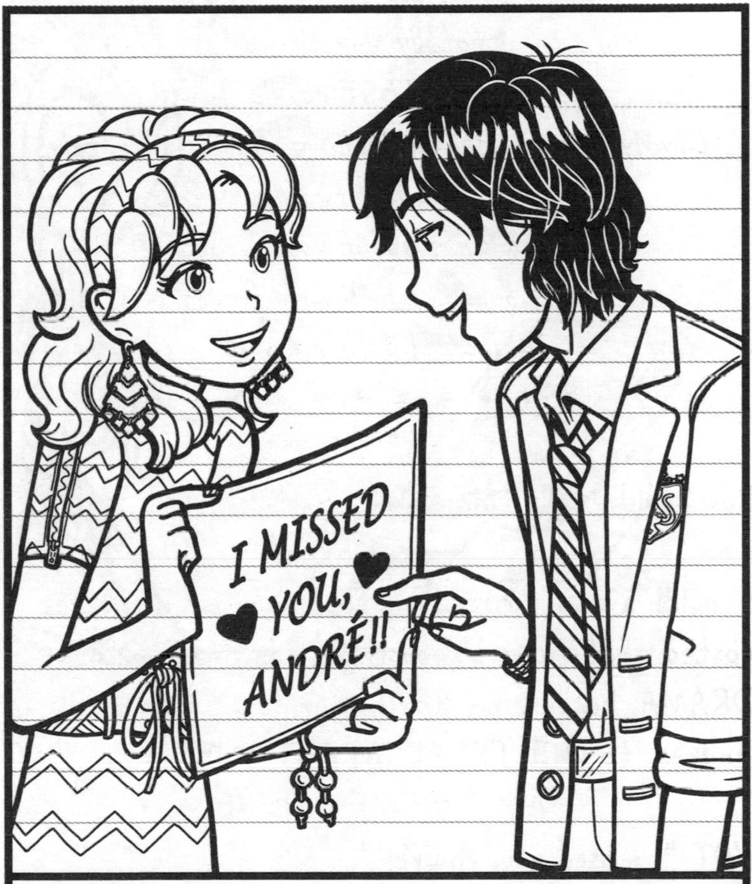
I MISSED YOU, ANDRÉ!!

Nikki & André hang out at WCD! Too CUTE!

* * * * * * * * * *
SelfieChic: ADORABLENESS!
LuvMyLipGloss: I heard they met while she was visiting
NHH. Maybe LOVE at first sight?!
Flawless: They are perfect together.
I totally ship them!
CheerGirl: CUTEST couple EVER!
LuvMyLipGloss: Hanging out with him is definitely
an upgrade from her two dorky BFFs.
Diva124: What about poor Brandon?
SelfieChic: Looks like he'll have to get over it.
Diva124: I'll take him ☺!
* * * * * * * * * *

How could people talk about my friends like that?!

I couldn't bear to read another comment! Whoever
posted that pic is obviously just trying to stir up
DRAMA, because my REAL sign said "Welcome,
Andrea, to WCD!!"

NOT "I missed you, André!!"

I sighed in frustration and clicked off that website.

141

That's when I realized my friends were STILL eagerly waiting for me to show them the e-mail I had mentioned.

"So, what do you need to show us?" Zoey asked. "Is it an e-mail from Trevor Chase?"

"OMG! It's an e-mail from the BAD BOYZ! RIGHT?!" Chloe shouted hysterically. "If it is, I think I'm going to DIE!"

JUST GREAT ☹!

Even my e-mail idea had turned into a HOT MESS!

"Listen, guys! I'm really sorry, but something just came up. I really need to GO! Right now! We can talk about this later, okay?" I said, trying to stay calm.

"Is something wrong, Nikki?!" Brandon asked, concerned.

"Um . . . NO! I just got an e-mail here . . . from my, um . . . MOM! And I have to go home to, uh . . .

babysit Brianna. Bye, guys!" I said as I quickly headed for the door.

"WHAT?!" Chloe and Zoey blinked in confusion.

"Wait a minute! Nikki, come back! Are you sure you're—" I didn't hear the rest of Brandon's question because I practically ran down the hall.

I had to get out of there before I burst into tears!

Right now I'm writing in my diary, trying to figure out how to fix this

DISASTER!

I'm pretty sure Chloe, Zoey, and Brandon hadn't seen that post yet.

If they had, I'm VERY sure they would have been upset enough to have mentioned it.

If/when Brandon finds out, I just hope he doesn't believe all the crazy gossip.

It might make him feel a little insecure (and extremely cruddy!) to hear rumors that André and I are a couple.

I already feel HORRIBLE for him!

And NOW I have to tell my BFFs about the trip to Paris AND the gossip about them online.

OH NO ☹! Daisy stole my peanut butter sandwich and got peanut butter EVERYWHERE! I actually had to change my clothes!

JUST GREAT ☹!! Now someone's ringing the doorbell.

OMG! I can't believe who's actually here!

It's . . .

BRANDON?!

☹!!

Brandon was at my front door! My first reaction
was . . .

NOOOOO ☹!!

I was pretty sure he'd seen the photo online
and had rushed over to my house to ask me
about it.

I now had the perfect opportunity to be a mature
and responsible adult and tell Brandon the TRUTH
about EVERYTHING!

Like . . .

André and I are MERELY friends.

I met him for the first time in my life less than
seventy-two hours ago.

I'm planning to ditch you, my BFFs, and the national Bad Boyz tour to hang out with him in Paris for two weeks!

Just ignore any photos you see of André and me.

And definitely don't believe any of the gossip.

Unfortunately, all of that sounded like a bunch of LIES. . . .

Even to ME ☹!
And I KNOW the truth!

So how could I expect Brandon to believe me?!!

The reality was that he probably wouldn't!

I didn't have a choice but to try to convince him.

I opened the door, grabbed Brandon's shoulders, and stared desperately into his eyes.

"Listen, Brandon! I know why you're here, and I don't blame you for being upset. But André and I are JUST friends! Nothing more! You gotta believe me!"

He just stared back at me, slightly surprised and totally confused. . . .

BRANDON STARES AT ME,
TOTALLY CONFUSED!

"Um . . . okay, Nikki. I think I understand. Does this mean that André is going to help out with Daisy's training session? Because today she's supposed to learn the sit and stay commands."

"OMG! It's Wednesday, and we have Daisy's training TODAY! So th-that's why you're here?!" I stammered.

"Um . . . is now a bad time?" Brandon asked.

"WHAT?! I mean . . . of COURSE not! I was just a little confused, that's all!" I babbled like an idiot. "Daisy is in the backyard."

"So what was all that stuff about André?" Brandon asked.

"Never mind! I'll grab us something to drink and meet you out back in a few minutes, okay?"

I could hardly believe Brandon was here for Daisy's second doggie obedience lesson!

<u>NOT</u> to grill me about my relationship with André and tell me what a hopelessly PATHETIC friend I am.

I actually felt totally RELIEVED!

Hey, why RUIN a fun evening hanging out with my crush?

So I decided <u>NOT</u> to bring up the trip to Paris, the Bad Boyz tour, or the online gossip.

Until . . .

LATER!

Since it was a warm evening, I made a delicious pitcher of ice-cold lemonade.

<u>What better way for Brandon and me to CHILLAX</u> <u>than with a cool, refreshing drink!</u>

<u>I was carrying the tray of lemonade over to Brandon</u> <u>when I encountered a series of unfortunate events. . . .</u>

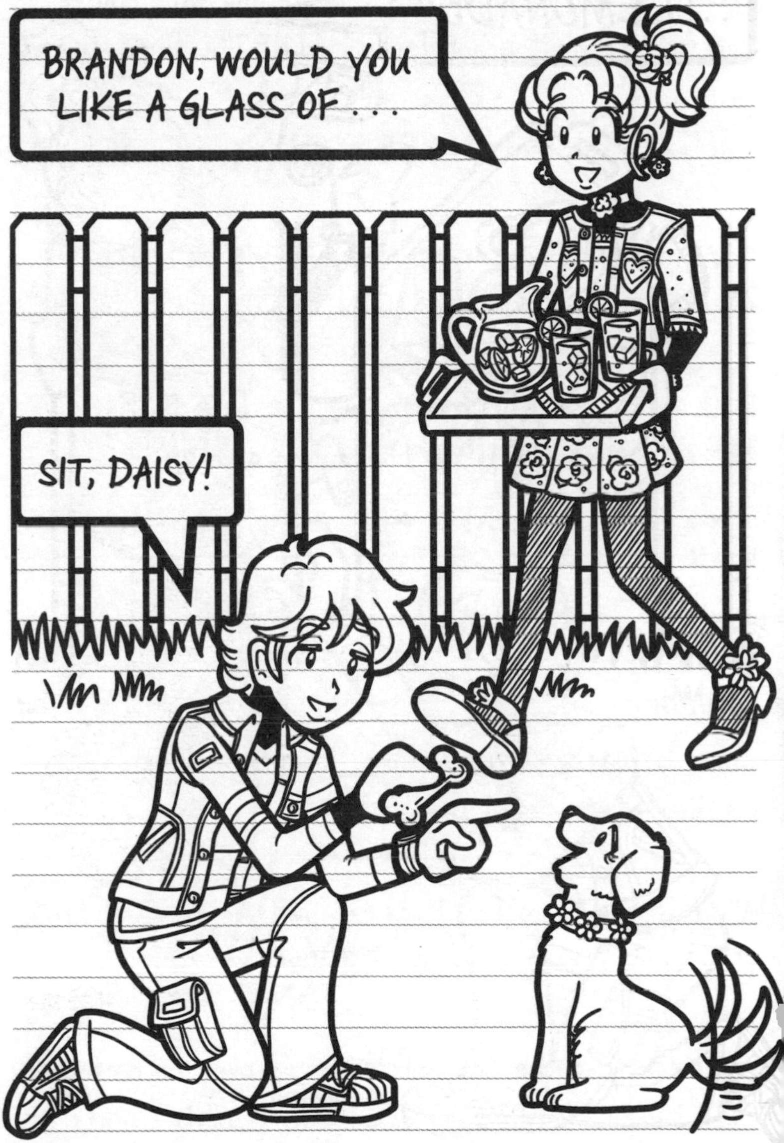
BRANDON, WOULD YOU LIKE A GLASS OF . . .
SIT, DAISY!

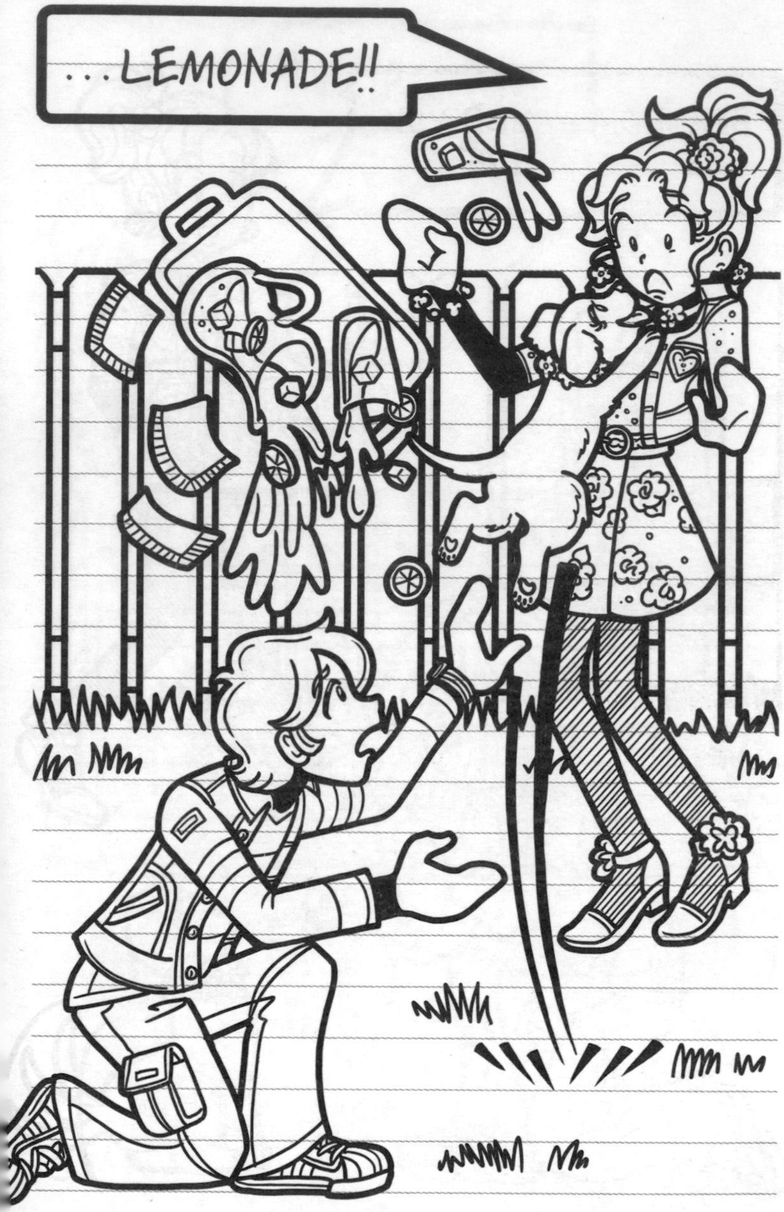
...LEMONADE!!

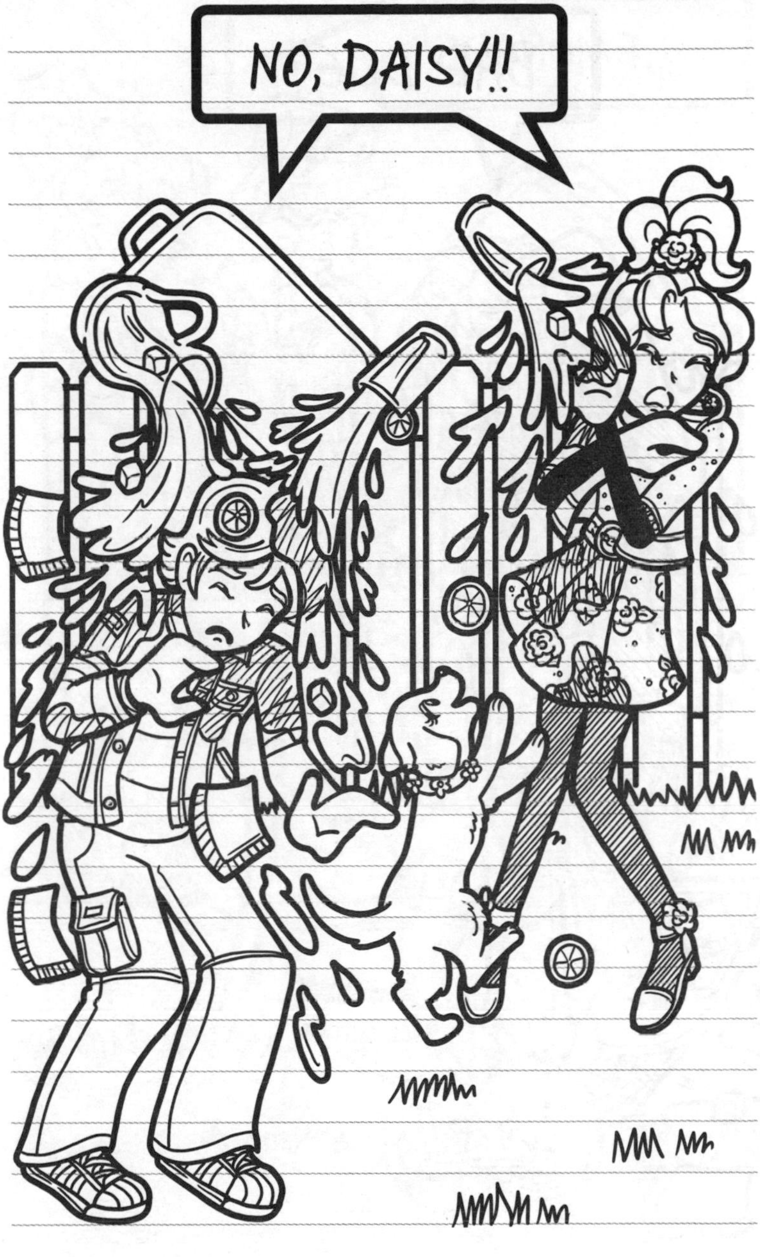
NO, DAISY!!

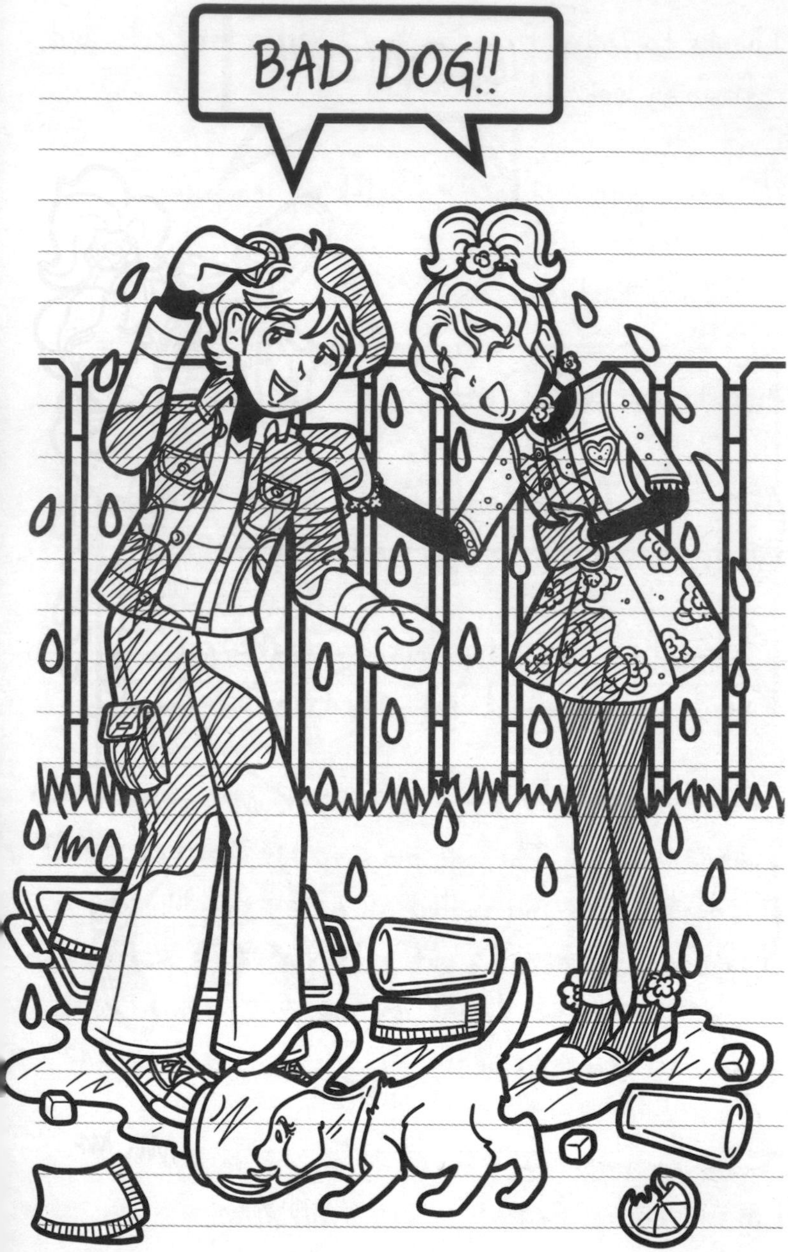
BAD DOG!!

Thanks to Daisy, Brandon and I had a very cold and refreshing lemonade SHOWER!

WE never got a chance to drink my lemonade.

But Daisy tasted it.

And she LOVED it!

After we'd finished with Daisy's lesson, I decided it was time to finally break the bad news.

"Listen, Brandon! I appreciate everything you've done for Daisy, but I really need to tell you—"

"Nikki, you DON'T have to THANK ME again!" Brandon smiled. Then he brushed his shaggy bangs out of his eyes and smiled at me all shy-like. "I really enjoy hanging out with you. As a matter of fact, I was wondering if you, um . . . wanted to go out to Queasy Cheesy for pizza this weekend?"

"Sure, Brandon! Of course. It would be fun," I answered very calmly.

But deep down inside I was elated and doing my Snoopy "happy dance." . . .

SQUEEEEEEE ☺!!

BRANDON ASKED ME TO HANG OUT AT QUEASY CHEESY!

We decided to text each other Saturday morning to arrange everything.

I know it's NOT actually a REAL date!

Since we're NOT actually a REAL couple!

YET!

But . . .

STILL☺!!

It's like really, really, really CLOSE to all of that without ACTUALLY being it.

So I decided NOT to RUIN the moment by bringing up other stuff.

Hey, when life gives you lemons, make lemonade!

Just try not to SPILL it all over your CRUSH!

I'm really lucky to have a friend like Brandon!

SQUEEEEEEE!!

☺!!

WEDNESDAY—9:00 P.M.
IN MY BEDROOM

This whole day has been one giant emotional ROLLER COASTER ☹!

Another photo was posted online about an hour ago. It was more gossip about André and me. . . .

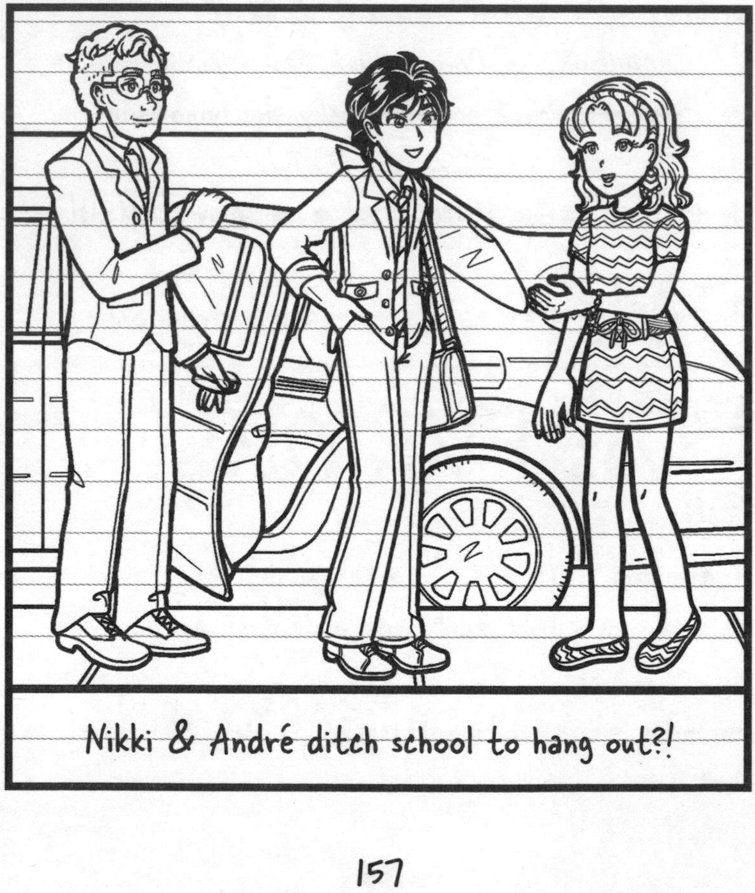

Nikki & André ditch school to hang out?!

* * * * * * * * * *

SelfieChic: Isn't this against the rules?!

LuvMyLipGloss: ONLY if they get caught ☺!

Diva124: Then they can do after-school detention
TOGETHER! How romantic!

CheerGirl: Where'd they go?

Flawless: Maybe to the CupCakery? In Paris! On his
family's private jet!

SelfieChic: I'm so JELLY!

LuvMyLipGloss: Poor André was probably trying
to get away from her tacky, annoying BFFs,
Chloe and Zoey!

* * * * * * * * * *

OMG!

I was FURIOUS!

André and I did **NOT** ditch school together!
He had simply left early for a dentist appointment.

I wonder who's posting this GARBAGE?!

Judging from the usernames, I can make a pretty good guess.

LuvMyLipGloss is probably MacKenzie, and SelfieChic is probably Tiffany from NHH.

I have no idea WHY they would do this to me.

Well, other than the fact that they both HATE my GUTS!!

The HUMILIATING part is that most of the students from WCD and NHH will probably read this stuff and believe it's TRUE!

It just occurred to me that posts like this are considered cyberbullying.

And both schools, WCD and NHH, have very strict rules against it.

Sometimes in life you have to do the right thing, even when it's difficult or unpopular.

Which means I need to PONDER a very COMPLEX and DIFFICULT question. . . .

WHY IS MY LIFE SUCH A GIANT BUCKET OF PUKE?!!

☹!!

THURSDAY, MAY 29—7:00 A.M.
IN MY BEDROOM

I just got out of bed thirty minutes ago, but I'm STILL totally EXHAUSTED, mostly due to excessive WORRY and SLEEP deprivation ☹!

My life would be PERFECT if I could sleep late, watch cartoons, chillax, eat yummy snacks, take a nap, AND go to school for only HALF a day.

Yes, I'll admit it. I WISH I was back in kindergarten! My life was SO simple then.

I checked my e-mail and there weren't any new posts about André and me. Thank goodness!

I DID receive that packet of info about the Paris trip. It said the flight is going to be seven and a half hours, which is really long.

But it's going to be a BREEZE compared to the HORRIFIC ninety-minute plane trip I took with Brianna last summer when we went to visit my aunt in Indiana.

It started with a really long wait in line to get through airport security to board the plane. Which meant wandering through a crowded maze, taking off our shoes, and then walking into that thing that looks like a space pod.

Brianna was bored out of her mind and sticking a wad of bubble gum up her nose (I am NOT lying!), when she suddenly pointed and screamed, "HEY, LOOK!! A PUPPY!"

Sure enough, there was a security guy with a German shepherd on a leash sniffing for drugs, bombs, or dangerous toiletries—whatever those dogs are trained to sniff for.

"Brianna, that dog is busy working," my dad explained. "So please don't bother it, honey."

In spite of my dad's warning, she quickly DOVE under the divider, rushed over to the dog, threw her arms around it, and gave it a big hug.

My mom gasped and I frantically dashed after Brianna.

Luckily, the dog just sniffed her and licked her. . . .

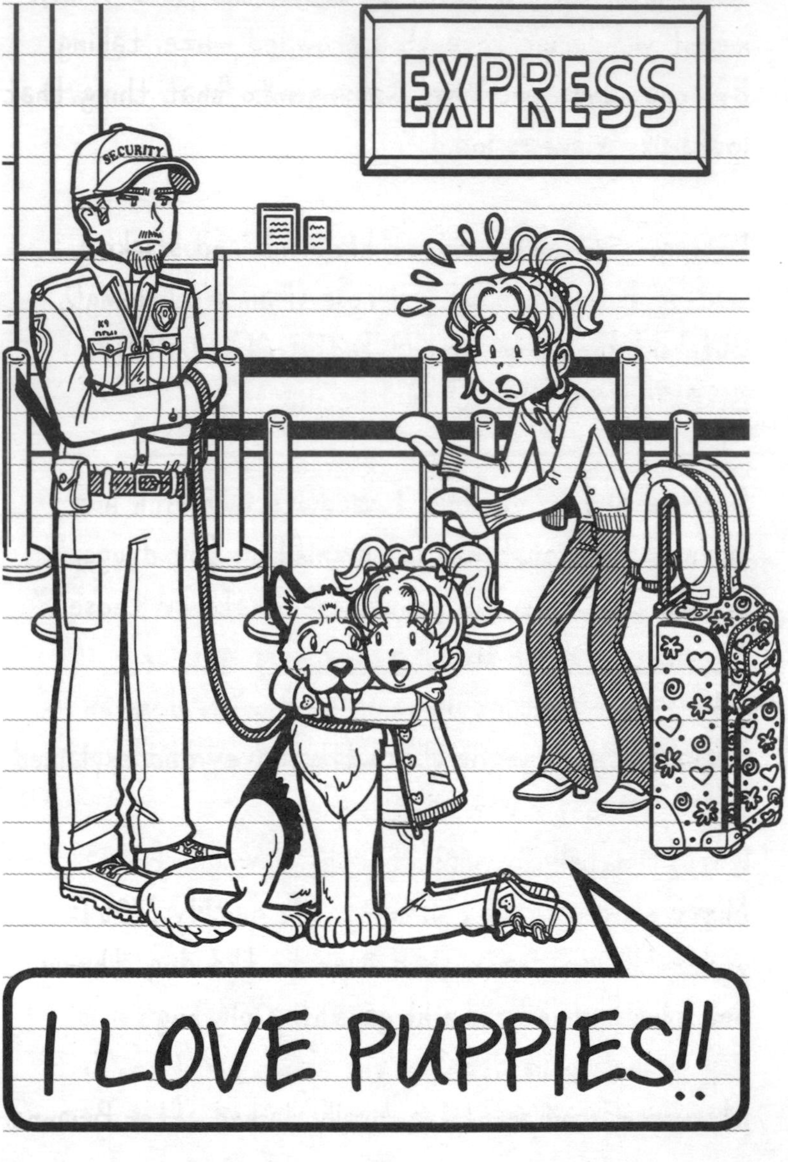
EXPRESS
SECURITY
K9
I LOVE PUPPIES!!

The grumpy security guy scowled at Brianna and said, "Step AWAY from the dog, miss!"

Brianna's eyes got huge. My parents froze. I quickly grabbed Brianna's hand.

"Sorry, sir! She's just a little kid," I apologized.

But he just glared at us. "BOTH OF YOU! STEP AWAY FROM THE DOG!" he shouted.

Brianna and I scrambled back to our spot in line while the dog just wagged his tail.

My bratty little sister had almost gotten us arrested by attack-hugging a security dog, and we hadn't even made it to the plane yet.

Unfortunately, it went totally downhill from there.

Since we had left the house at 6:00 a.m., I was hoping she would sleep on the plane, but I couldn't have been more wrong!

She was so hyped up on sugar from an overpriced airport breakfast of doughnuts and hot chocolate that she probably wasn't going to sleep for at least a week. (Thanks a lot, MOM ☹!)

To make matters worse, this was Brianna's very first trip on a plane.

And, unfortunately, we didn't have four seats all together in the same row, because each row had only three seats.

My parents sat together, and I was stuck sitting with Brianna a few rows behind them.

Brianna demanded the window seat. So I was trapped between her and this businessman who kept on elbowing me as he typed on his laptop.

"Why aren't we flying?" she asked two seconds after we sat down.

"Brianna, people are still boarding the plane," I explained. "We'll be leaving soon, okay?!"

"How about now? Is it time yet? When are we going to flyyyyyyy??!!" she complained.

Mr. Laptop Guy was straight up trying to kill us WITH HIS EYES.

I mean, I wanted Brianna to shut up too! But why was he giving ME the EVIL EYE?!

Once everyone was seated, the flight attendant started her speech about what to do when the plane CRASHES into the OCEAN.

I'm not going to lie! That speech always makes me a little nervous. So I kind of understood when Brianna started to freak out.

But my little sister took FREAKING OUT to a whole new level!

"Is my seat belt tight enough? Promise you'll do my air mask first, Nikki! A WATER landing?! WHERE'S MY LIFE VEST?!!" Brianna panicked.

Then she climbed OUT of her seat and crawled underneath it, even though the plane was already taxiing on the runway.

OMG! I almost had a heart attack when Brianna pulled out the life vest that was attached to the bottom of her seat.

"Hey! She can't do that!" Mr. Laptop Guy huffed, looking up from his computer.

"Yeah, well, you're not supposed to be on your laptop during takeoff, either!" I shot back.

But I just said it inside my head, so no one else heard it but me.

I pulled Brianna back into her seat and grabbed her seat belt.

Okay. So have you ever tried to put a seat belt on a child who is KICKING, SCREAMING, and having a TEMPER TANTRUM while wearing a LIFE VEST aboard an AIRPLANE?! . . .

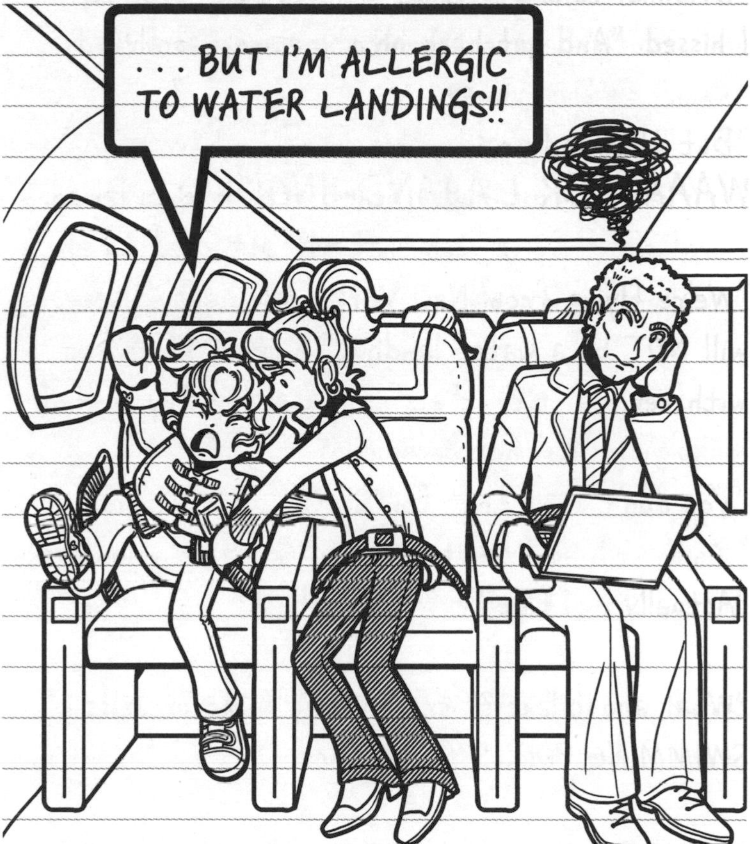
. . . BUT I'M ALLERGIC TO WATER LANDINGS!!

BRIANNA HAS A COMPLETE MELTDOWN ON THE PLANE!

Well, I HAVE!!

And it's pretty much . . . IMPOSSIBLE!

"Brianna, take off that LIFE VEST NOW!"
I hissed. "And get back into your seat belt!"

"But that lady said we're going to have a
WAAA-TER LAAAND-ING!" she screamed.

"We're flying from New York to Indiana. There
will NOT be a water landing," I tried to reason
with her.

"You don't know that for SURE!" she whined.

"Actually . . . I do!"

"What about lakes?! And rivers?! And . . . and . . .
SWIMMING POOLS?!" she cried.

Okay, so maybe my sister had a point, but still.

I was like, SORRY, BRIANNA!

CRASHING into a SWIMMING POOL is way better
than ANOTHER MINUTE stuck sitting next to
YOU on this PLANE!

"Look, Brianna, if you chill out, I'll let you play Princess Sugar Plum: Adventures on Baby Unicorn Island on my cell phone, okay?!"

But she didn't answer because right then the plane lifted off the ground. And our ascent into the air felt a lot like a roller coaster going up a huge hill.

That's when Brianna started to SCREAM! At the top of her lungs!

"Would you PLEASE tell her to be quiet?!" Mr. Laptop Guy grumbled.

"Sorry," I mumbled. "Brianna, hey! Look at me! We're okay! You wanted to fly! We're flying! Like . . . like fairies! Like . . . unicorns!"

"Unicorns don't FLY!" a woman muttered behind me. She was NOT helping. Thanks for NOTHING, lady!

(And I KNOW unicorns don't fly, but this was a VERY stressful situation, okay?)

"Um, is she all right?" a flight attendant said, gripping the top of Mr. Laptop Guy's seat.

I don't think she was supposed to be walking around yet, but Brianna's screams were hard to ignore.

"NOT really!" I sighed.

"Is she actually . . . wearing her LIFE VEST?!" the attendant asked in disbelief.

DUH!! This lady had a really strong grasp of the OBVIOUS!!

"I'd like a different seat," Mr. Laptop Guy snarled.

"Brianna, honey, why are you screaming?" asked my mom, who was now standing up in her row.

"Ma'am, PLEASE sit down! NOW!" the flight attendant snapped at her.

"THAT is MY daughter!" Mom shot back.

171

Suddenly Brianna stopped screaming and pointed out the window. "Wow! Cotton candy clouds?!"

After that, Mr. Laptop Guy switched seats with my mom, and Brianna only SCREAMED again when the plane ride got a little bumpy. . . .

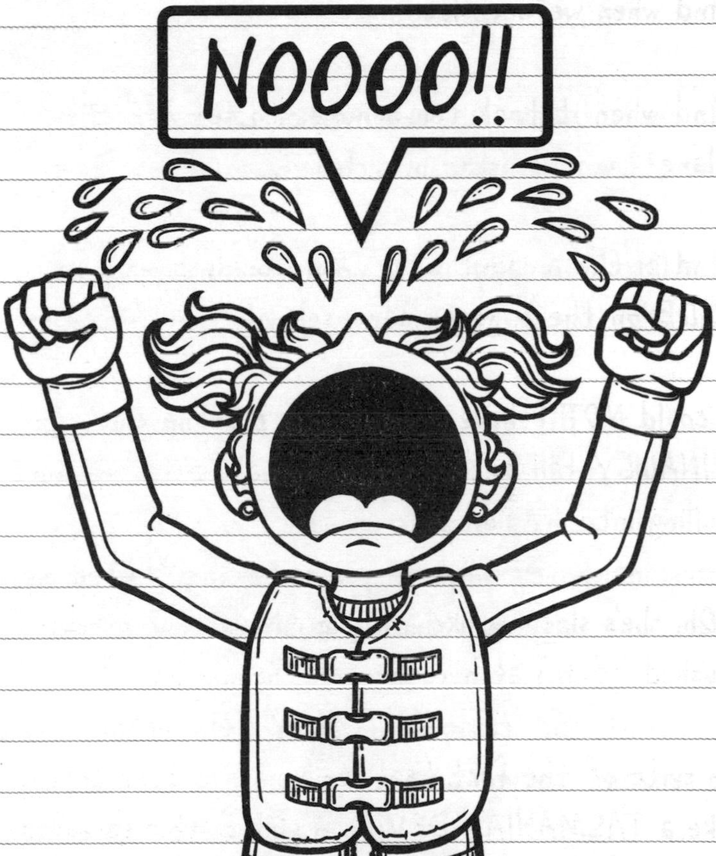
NOOOO!!

And when someone flushed the toilet on the plane.

And when the flight attendant offered her apple juice because the airline didn't serve Princess Sugar Plum punch.

And when we were landing.

And when it took ten minutes to get off the plane.

And in the airport when Dad wouldn't let her RIDE on the baggage carousel with the suitcases.

I could NOT believe the moment Brianna chose to FINALLY fall asleep. In the rental car, as we were pulling into my aunt's driveway!

"Oh, she's sleeping like a little ANGEL!" my aunt gushed, gazing at her through the window.

In spite of the fact that Brianna had been acting like a TASMANIAN DEVIL in pink Barbie sneakers, my mom actually AGREED with her!

That's when I totally LOST IT!

"REALLY?! If Brianna is an ANGEL, then maybe she can FLY herself home! SORRY, people! But I will NOT be sitting next to HER on the return flight!"

But I just said that inside my head, so no one else heard it but me.

Hey, I really LOVE my little sister!

It's just that sometimes I can't help but wonder what it would be like to be an ONLY child.

Anyway, I've finally decided to break the news to Brandon about the trip to Paris when we hang out at Queasy Cheesy this weekend.

Then maybe we can both meet Chloe and Zoey at the CupCakery and tell them everything.

I've decided not to worry about those stupid photos for now.

André's last day here at WCD is tomorrow, and then he'll be going back to NHH.

So, it will be impossible for anyone to post new photos after that since we won't be around each other anymore.

I guess those HATERS will have to find something else to do.

Thank goodness all this photo drama will be over in
TWO MORE DAYS!

I just hope my BFFs don't see them before then.

Fingers crossed!

I already feel like a humongous weight has been lifted off my shoulders.

☺!!

THURSDAY—12:20 P.M.
AT MY LOCKER

Well, my day is pretty much RUINED ☹!

A new photo was posted two hours ago. . . .

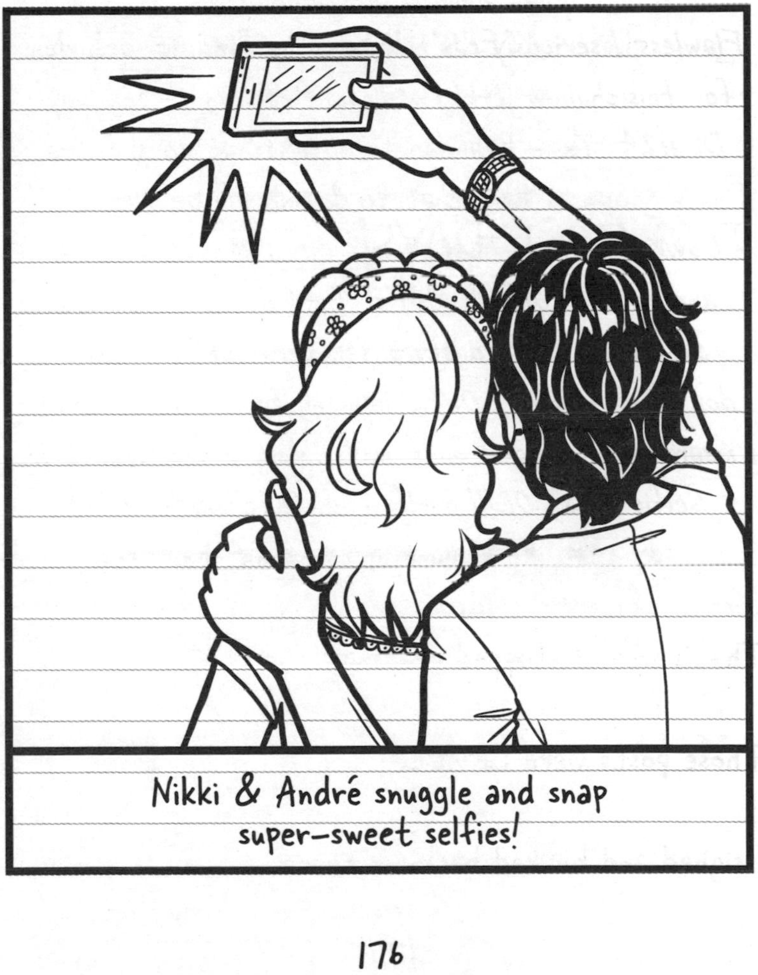

Nikki & André snuggle and snap super-sweet selfies!

* * * * * * * * * *

CheerGirl: Awww! Don't they make
a picture-perfect couple?
LuvMyLipGloss: Nikki STILL denies they're an item,
tho. Nikki, we see you, girl!
SelfieChic: Right! She's not fooling anybody!
That chick is SO scandalous!
Flawless: I seriously can't believe she dropped Brandon
for this shallow jerk! I'm Team Brandon all the way!
Diva124: Team Brandon for life! What does André
have that he doesn't?
LuvMyLipGloss: That's easy! He's French, he's fine,
and he has tons of MONEY! All Brandon has is a
cute smile and a dusty old camera. And I totally
don't get why he LOVES hanging around stray dogs!
I mean the 4-legged ones, not Chloe, Zoey, and Nikki.
SelfieChic: LOL!!! Girlfriend, that was SHADY!

* * * * * * * * * *

That's when I stopped reading.

Those posts were CRUEL!!

I sighed and blinked back my tears.

Then I studied the photo carefully, trying my best to remember when André and I may have taken any selfies together.

Based on the outfit I was wearing, this had to have been taken on Tuesday.

That's when I suddenly remembered that Chloe, Zoey, André, and I had taken a selfie together on that day.

But it appeared that Chloe and Zoey had been completely cropped out of the photo.

Obviously, someone wanted it to look like André and I were taking selfies together because we were totally into each other.

Which is a BIG FAT LIE!!

I was SO . . .

ANGRY !

But not nearly as ANGRY as I was about the photo that was just posted ten minutes ago. . . .

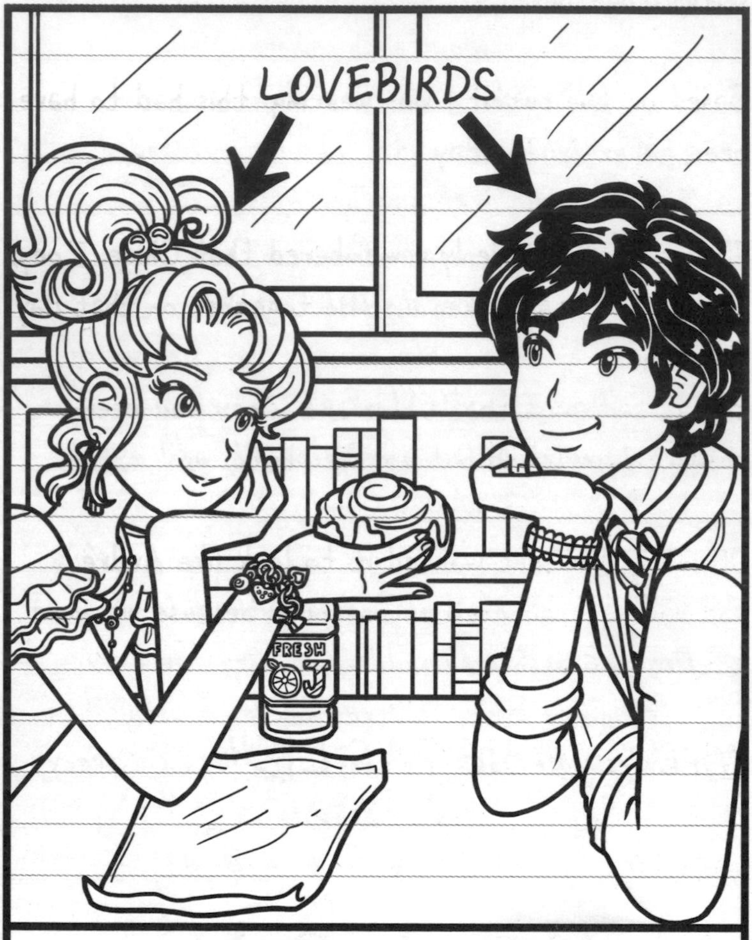
LOVEBIRDS
FRESH
OJ

Nikki & André share a pastry!

* * * * * * * * * *

SelfieChic: OMG! This is SOOO romantic!

Dival24: Well, it's quite obvious they're serious
about each other.

Flawless: Nikki! How could you?!

LuvMyLipGloss: Just wait until Brandon
finds out. Watching her messy love life
unfold will be like watching a train wreck.
I am totally LOVING IT!

SelfieChic: Me too! Things are getting good!
I've got my bowl of popcorn ready!

LuvMyLipGloss: I've got candy and my
3-D glasses on! LOL!

CheerGirl: Um . . . I think you two are enjoying
this a little too much.

Dival24: Why am I suddenly hungry for a warm
cinnamon bun with cream cheese frosting?

Flawless: Me too! Let's meet at the CupCakery
after school.

* * * * * * * * * *

I stopped reading and shoved my cell phone back into
my purse.

I wanted to . . .

SCREEEEEAM ☹!!

André and I each had our OWN cinnamon roll!

But for some reason, only ONE was shown in the photo!

MINE ☹!!

There was NO WAY we were just sitting there in the library like a bride and groom sharing a piece of wedding cake!

Hey, I barely even KNOW the guy!!

To make things even worse, it feels like the entire school is GOSSIPING about me.

Well, most of the kids in the CCP (Cute, Cool, and Popular) clique, anyway.

MacKenzie and her friends were whispering about me while I was at my locker.

My stomach feels so QUEASY, I could throw up on MacKenzie's really cute gold designer platform sandals.

If I wasn't so WORRIED about Brandon seeing those photos, assuming the worst, getting his feelings hurt, and then NEVER speaking to me again, I'd rush down to the office, call my mom, and go HOME!

But instead I plan to go straight to BIO and WARN Brandon about those photos!

Before it's too late!

☹!

THURSDAY—3:30 P.M.
IN THE JANITOR'S CLOSET

Right now I'm in the janitor's closet, writing this and trying not to have a complete MELTDOWN!

OMG! MacKenzie Hollister is . . .

PURE EVIL ☹!

HOW evil is she?!!

She's SO evil that if I was in the HOSPITAL, she'd UNPLUG my LIFE SUPPORT to charge her CELL PHONE!

As soon as I finished my last diary entry, I grabbed my books, stopped by André's locker (hey, he's part of my job duties!), and rushed straight to bio.

But, unfortunately, I had arrived just seconds TOO LATE. . . .

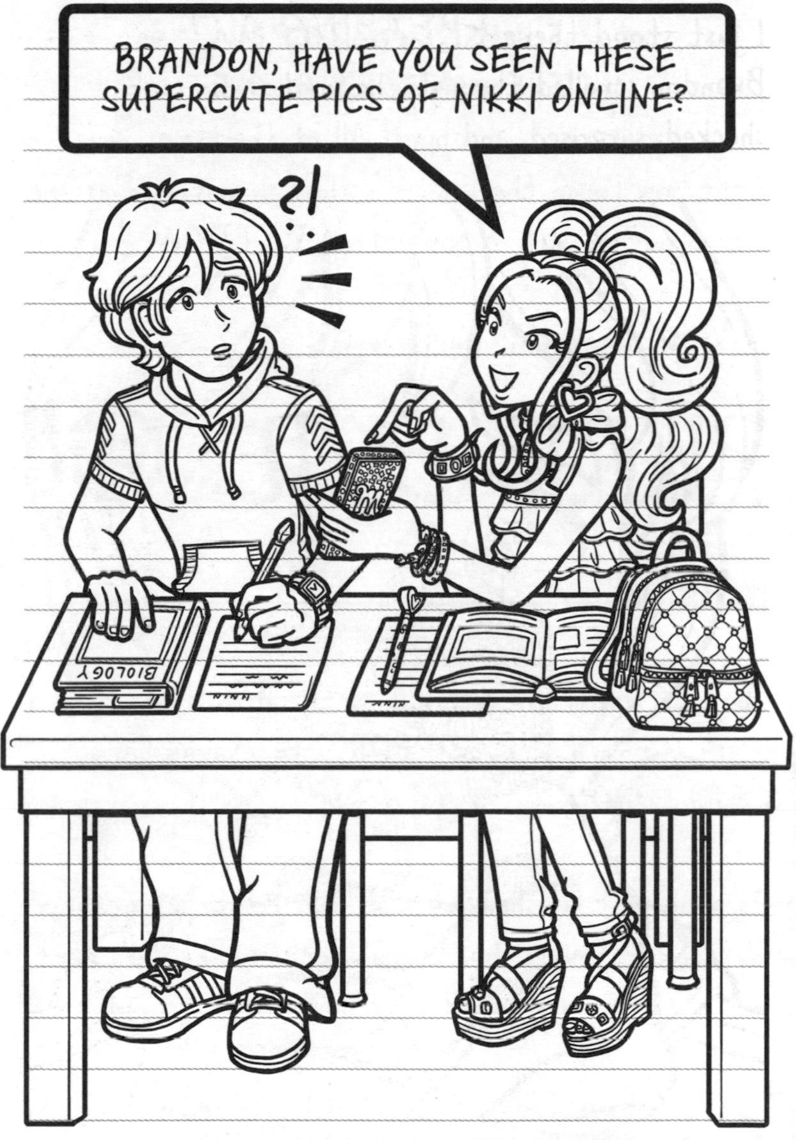
BRANDON, HAVE YOU SEEN THESE SUPERCUTE PICS OF NIKKI ONLINE?
?!
BIOLOGY

MACKENZIE SHOWS BRANDON
THE PICS OF ANDRÉ AND ME!

I just stood there FREAKING OUT as Brandon scrolled through the photos. He looked shocked, surprised, and hurt! All at the same time. . . .

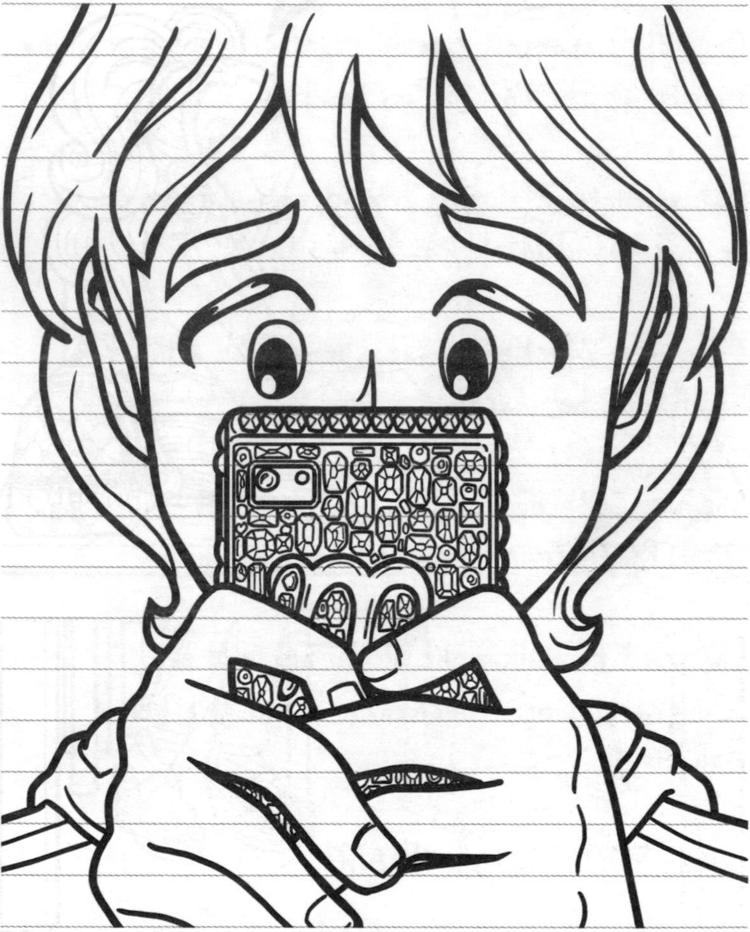

BRANDON LOOKS AT THE PICS!

Right then all I wanted to do was dig a really deep hole right next to my desk, CRAWL into it, and DIE!!

Once class started, I could practically feel Brandon staring at the back of my head.

But whenever I turned around to make eye contact, he just gazed blankly at his bio book.

Of course MacKenzie sat there with a big fat SMIRK on her face.

She was SO proud of herself for pretty much DESTROYING my friendship with Brandon.

I wanted to walk right up to her and say, "Congratulations, MacKenzie!" and give her a high five!

In the FACE. With a CHAIR!

Just kidding ☺!

NOT 😟!

Seriously! That girl is lucky I'm a very peaceful and nonviolent person.

I just totally ignored her when she started EYEBALLING me all EVIL-LIKE. . . .

MACKENZIE, EYEBALLING ME
ALL EVIL-LIKE

I mean, WHO does THAT?!!

As soon as class was over, Brandon grabbed his backpack and quickly strode past me and out of the room.

Practically everyone in class had heard the latest gossip and was STARING at us.

"Brandon, wait! I really need to talk to you!" I said, following him out into the hall. "Privately. Can we meet at your locker after school?"

"Actually, Nikki, I'm supposed to work on the Fuzzy Friends website with some volunteers after school. I've been staying up really late all week, and it's not even half finished. And now my homework is piling up," he said, staring at the floor.

I had to admit, he looked exhausted.

I hadn't noticed the dark circles under his eyes until now.

"Well, how about tomorrow morning?" I asked.

"I'm coming to school an hour early tomorrow. But I'll be busy in the library, trying to finish up all my homework that was due YESTERDAY and TODAY," he muttered in frustration.

"Can you at least give me a minute or two?" I practically begged. "I mean, if you have time. . . ."

"The real question is, do YOU have time?" Brandon said, finally looking at me. "Apparently, you've been really busy lately with your NEW school project!"

"School project?! WHAT school project?" I asked, confused.

Suddenly Brandon narrowed his eyes and stared behind me.

"Here, Nicole," André said, handing me my backpack. "We'd better get going or we'll be late for class. Oh . . . hello, Brandon."

"NICOLE?! Who's . . . Nicole?" Brandon asked, staring at me, then André, and then back at me. "Never mind. I gotta go. Later."

He sighed, thrust his hands deep into his pockets, turned, and trudged away.

"What's wrong with HIM?" André shrugged. "He's acting like his BEST FRIEND just DIED!"

"Actually, SHE DID!" I sighed, blinking back tears as I watched Brandon disappear down the hall.

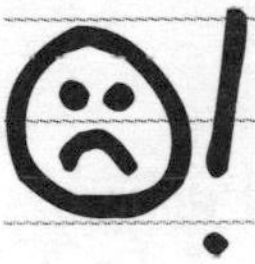

FRIDAY, MAY 30—7:00 A.M.
IN MY BEDROOM

OMG! All that drama in BIO yesterday was . . .

HORRIFIC!

I had no idea Brandon was feeling overwhelmed.

He's been spending so much time working on the Fuzzy Friends project that he's fallen behind on his homework and started to struggle at school.

And if all that isn't EXHAUSTING enough, he's ALSO been coming to MY house TWICE a week to train Daisy.

I honestly can't blame Brandon for feeling a little insecure about OUR friendship when I've been spending so much time with André.

Those pics of André and me probably felt like a huge SLAP in the face and pushed him over the edge.

And now I can't get him out of my mind! He looked so SAD just sitting there alone. . . .

BRANDON AT SCHOOL

Obviously, whoever posted those photos is trying to hurt him AND damage our friendship.

But I have to admit, I'm ALSO responsible. I was SO self-absorbed in my own little world, worrying about my own personal problems, that I'd basically ignored Brandon.

I felt really AWFUL that I'd let my friend down like that ☹! I didn't have a choice but to try to make it up to him, some way, somehow.

Brandon had asked me to draw some of the puppies that had recently been placed by Fuzzy Friends, but instead I'd gotten sidetracked with my student ambassador duties.

So last night, after I completed my homework, I worked on those puppy drawings for HOURS! I didn't finish until after midnight.

I realize I'm the LAST person Brandon wants to talk to right now. So I decided to write him a short letter.

I plan to give it to him along with the puppy drawings when I see him at school today. . . .

Hi,

Please let me know what you think about the four pics. I think they're DEFINITELY going to get a lot of attention online!

BTW, can we hang out later to talk? It's about something kind of important. Okay, VERY important! So important that I've been trying to tell you about it for the past week but couldn't.

It was hard finding the right time since we've both been insanely busy. So let's hang out this Saturday! Does 1:00 p.m. at Queasy Cheesy work for you? Shoot me a text and let me know. After the stressful week we've had, it'll be fun to just eat and chillax with you!

Nikki

I folded the letter, tucked it into an envelope, and scribbled Brandon's name on it.

It's hard to believe that today is André's last day at WCD! The week went by so fast. In spite of all the DRAMA his visit created, I really like him and consider him a new friend. But, unfortunately,

I'm feeling more confused than ever about having to choose between the Bad Boyz tour and the trip to Paris. So I decided to write a letter to André. . . .

Hi,

I can't believe how fast this week went by! The good news is that you survived it ☺.

Now comes the awkward part. . . . I wanted to let you know that I'm still thinking about what we discussed. And, to be honest, I just don't know how I feel yet.

Having to choose between two things I really care about is A LOT of pressure! Half of me wants to stick with what's familiar and makes me happy. And the other half of me wants something new, adventurous, and exciting.

I'm SO torn!! Maybe I'm afraid of disappointing people. Or maybe I'm just scared of making a commitment. I'm going to need more time to figure stuff out.

I hope you understand! When I make my final decision, I'll definitely let you know. Regardless of

what I decide, I'd still like to be friends if that's okay with you! Hopefully, I'll see you around.

Nikki

P.S. Here is that gift card for a FREE Queasy Cheesy pizza. ENJOY ☺!

I tucked the letter into a second envelope and scribbled André's name on it. Then I stuck both letters and the drawings into a folder and placed everything inside my backpack.

It feels like I'm FINALLY getting my life back under control. The good news is that on Monday my schedule will be back to normal and I'll have two classes and lunch with Chloe and Zoey again! SQUEEEE ☺!

OMG! They're NOT going to believe all the SHADY stuff MacKenzie did to me this week. I can't wait to tell them.

But, most important, I'm REALLY going to need my BFFs to help me patch things up with Brandon. ☺!!

FRIDAY—9:55 A.M.
AT MY LOCKER

I arrived at school this morning fifteen minutes early, just as I had planned.

I was hoping it was enough time to find Brandon and give him the artwork and the letter.

It was the first step toward rebuilding our friendship.

Yesterday he'd mentioned that he was going to be in the library trying to catch up on homework, so my plan was to start there.

Since it was a warm and breezy day, I decided to stop in the girls' bathroom just to make sure my hair wasn't windblown and I didn't have any food stuck in my teeth.

But as soon as I stepped inside, my stomach started to churn so badly, I thought for sure I was going to lose my taco breakfast bagel. . . .

WHY?! Because MacKenzie was at the mirror, slathering on nine layers of lip gloss. . .

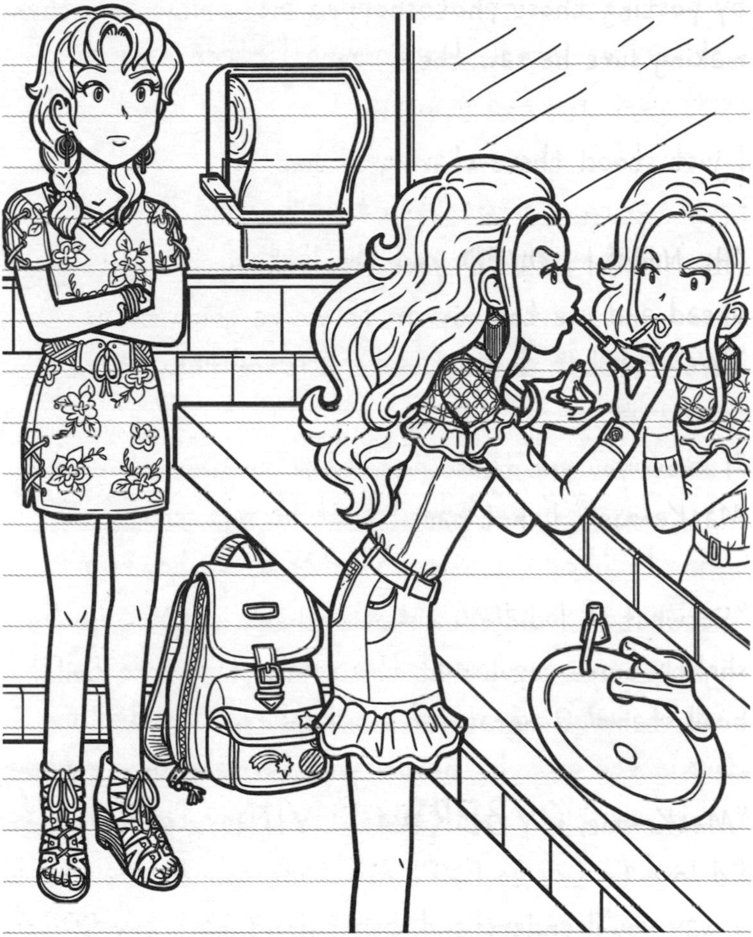

I RUN INTO MACKENZIE
IN THE GIRLS' BATHROOM!

I didn't have any proof! But I was VERY sure she had tried to destroy my friendship with Brandon by posting those photoshopped pics online and then making sure he saw them.

I just stood there staring at her.

"Hi, Nikki! I LOVED your pics online! Go right ahead and use the mirror. If you're going to be TWO-FACED, at least make ONE of them pretty!"

"I know you put those pics online, so just admit it, MacKenzie!" I shot back.

"So what if I did! You should thank me. Now you're slightly more popular at this school than the toilet bowl stains! Congratulations, hon!"

"MacKenzie, CYBERBULLYING is WRONG! I'd love to try to EXPLAIN that concept to you in a way you'd understand, but I don't have any SOCK PUPPETS, CHEERIOS, and CRAYONS!"

MacKenzie turned and glared at me.

"Nikki, I am SO sick of you! Everything is handed to you on a silver platter, and you don't deserve any of it. I should be going on that Bad Boyz tour! And as soon as you dump your little friends to go hang out in Paris with André, that lead singer SPOT is all MINE! To be honest, I don't get what André or Brandon see in you. They should be obsessed with ME! I guess you're just irresistibly ADORABLE and DUMB like a little puppy!"

"Wait a minute. You're doing all this just to go on tour?! Do you even realize you're HURTING other people? Like my FRIENDS?!" I exclaimed.

"Sorry, Nikki! You must be mistaking me for someone who actually CARES! Is your little bathroom DRAMA going to have an intermission soon? Because I need to pee!"

It was like MacKenzie had NOT heard a single word I'd said. She was HOPELESS!

"Listen, Nikki! Could you do me a big favor and go stand inside a stall until I leave? Your ugly dress

is clashing with my lip gloss, and it's giving me a MIGRAINE!"

When you encounter a big PILE of CRAZY, sometimes it's best not to waste your time and energy trying to REASON with it. So I turned and walked away.

It was WAY more important that I try to find Brandon and give him the artwork.

But by the time I got to the library door, I suddenly realized I didn't have my backpack.

JUST GREAT ☹!!

I had left it in the BATHROOM!!

With . . . MACKENZIE HOLLISTER ☹!!

I turned around and sprinted down the hall, back to the bathroom. I just KNEW my backpack was history!

But MacKenzie must not have noticed it under the counter, because it was STILL there. . . .

I FIND MY BACKPACK!!

I looked inside and saw my purse, phone, and book.

My artwork was in my folder, and when I peeked inside the envelopes, my letters were still there.

WHEW ☺!!

I hurried back to the library again.

My heart actually skipped a beat when I spotted Brandon sitting at a back table, hunched over a notebook.

"What's up, Brandon?" I said cheerfully. "I have a surprise! It's for the Fuzzy Friends website."

He didn't answer or even look at me. Maybe he was more upset at me than I thought.

I just froze, not having the slightest idea what to do next.

"Um, Brandon, are you okay?"

That's when I finally realized he was even more exhausted than yesterday. The poor guy should've just stayed home from school.

I didn't have the heart to disturb him. So I tiptoed over to him and very quietly left my puppy drawings and my letter on the table right next to his notebook. . . .

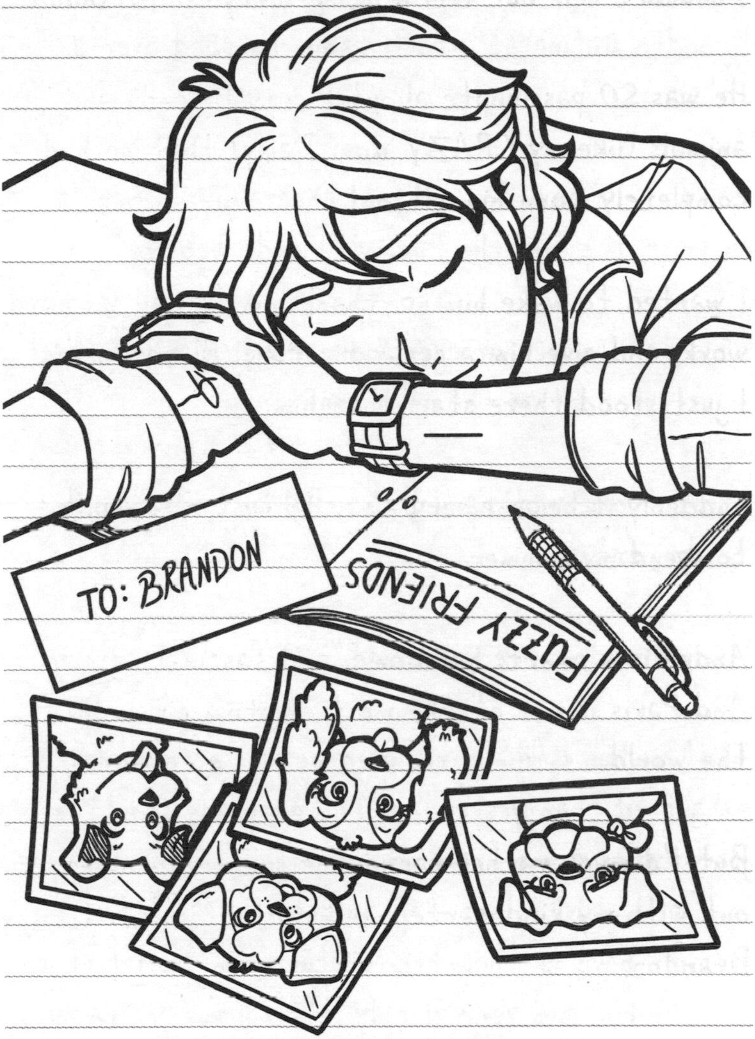
TO: BRANDON
FUZZY FRIENDS

AN EXHAUSTED BRANDON,
SLEEPING IN THE LIBRARY!

I couldn't help but feel a little sorry for Brandon.

He was SO passionate about Fuzzy Friends and animals (like my CRAZY dog, Daisy) that he had completely worn himself out.

I wanted to wake him up, thank him for all his hard work, and give him a great big HUG. But I didn't. I just stood there staring at him.

Suddenly it became very clear to me how I wanted to spend my summer.

André is a smart, handsome, and fascinating guy. And Paris is one of the most exciting cities in the world.

But I'd much rather spend the summer hanging out with my kindhearted and dorky CRUSH, Brandon.

I can't wait to tell him just how I feel.

☺!!

SATURDAY, MAY 31—11:15 P.M.
IN MY BEDROOM

Okay, I think this is probably going to be my LONGEST diary entry EVER!

First of all, I didn't have the slightest idea if Brandon was even going to show up at Queasy Cheesy.

I'd asked him in my letter to text me to let me know if Saturday at 1:00 p.m. was a good time, but he never responded.

I was starting to worry that maybe he was still MAD at me or something. Although I couldn't blame him.

If I had treated MYSELF the way I'd treated Brandon, I definitely would have UNFRIENDED myself on FACEBOOK!

I arrived at Queasy Cheesy fifteen minutes early and was a nervous wreck. But soon 1:00 p.m. had come and gone.

That's when it became VERY clear.

MY CRUSH HAD DITCHED ME!! . . .

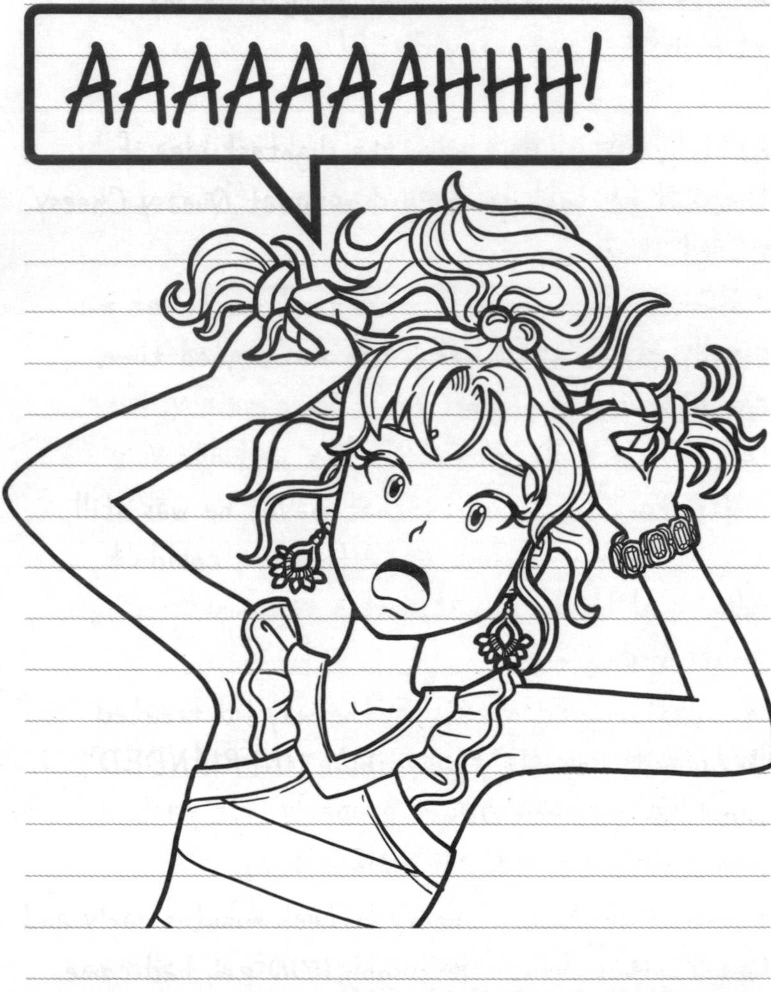
AAAAAAAHHH!

ME, HAVING A VERY SERIOUS CRUSH-ITIS CRISIS

OMG! My **WORST** fear had come true.

I was suffering from that very dangerous crush–itis complication that Chloe and Zoey had WARNED me about!

I totally lost it and had a massive meltdown right there at my table. While everyone in the restaurant stared at me.

Finally, my waitress came over and smiled at me sympathetically. "Dear, you've been waiting here for quite a while. Would you like to place your order now?"

"Um . . . I think I'll just wait a few minutes longer," I muttered.

"Well, suit yourself, honey. But, personally, I DON'T think HE'S coming! You're probably just wasting your time," she said, and walked away.

I could **NOT** believe my waitress actually said that to me! _HOW RUDE_ ☹!!

WHY was she all up in my personal business like that?! I had never seen that lady before in my life!

I seriously thought about complaining to the management.

But then I remembered the Queasy Cheesy pizza gift cards that my dad had given me.

If I made a big stink about the waitress, it might end up damaging my dad's business relationship.

I'd completely given up hope and was looking at the takeout menu when I heard a familiar voice. . . .

"SORRY I'M LATE! I HOPE I DIDN'T KEEP YOU WAITING TOO LONG!"

Lucky me! I won't be leaving here in tears with a broken heart, munching on a takeout order of wing-dings after all, I thought happily ☺!

I looked up, HOPING to see my crush, Brandon. . . .

209

HELLO, NICOLE! IT'S NICE TO SEE YOU AGAIN!

The CupCakery

CONGRATS!!

BUT IT WAS ANDRÉ!

"Oh! Hi, André!" I said, trying not to sound as disappointed as I felt. "How are you? Um . . . what are YOU doing here?"

"Well, I was invited by a very special person!" he said, with a huge smile plastered across his face. "I'm here to wish her happiness and help celebrate her success!"

I couldn't help but notice the balloons and CupCakery box he was holding.

"So, you're here for a party or something?" I asked, a little confused.

André seemed a little too old to be invited to a kiddie-themed birthday party at Queasy Cheesy. But hey, who was I to judge?!

Or maybe he was here for his OWN birthday.

"OMG, André! Is it YOUR birthday today? If so, the least I can do is, um . . . buy you some Queasy Cheesy tokens for the game room. I need to warn you that the popcorn is a little stale, and, whatever you do, DON'T go into the ball pit. My little sister, Brianna, said a kid threw up in it the last time we were here."

André laughed. "You have such a wicked sense of humor, Nicole. But it's NOT my birthday. Oh, I almost forgot. Here! These are for YOU!"

He handed me the mini bouquet of balloons and the CupCakery box.

"I brought you French pastries! They're just a small taste of the totally AMAZING things you'll experience during a summer in PARIS!" he said wistfully.

"André, you DIDN'T have to do this! I was just doing my job as a student ambassador. I mean, it was MANDATORY. I didn't have a choice."

"But I DO have a choice! And I want you to have them." He smiled. "I'll go ask the waitress for plates. You should try a chocolate croissant while they're still warm. I'll be right back!"

"But what about that party you said you were invited to? I don't want you to miss it because of me," I protested as he walked away and disappeared in the crowded restaurant.

Curious, I opened the box and peeked inside at the pastries. They looked delish!

I was startled by a voice directly behind me, and I turned to see a guy staring at me. . . .

NIKKI?! WHAT'S UP? I DIDN'T EXPECT TO SEE YOU HERE!

IT WAS BRANDON!!

"OMG! Brandon, you're HERE!" I gushed. "I'm SO happy to see you!"

"Thanks. I'm happy to see you, too!" He blushed.

"But what are you doing with that pizza? I've barely looked at the menu," I said.

"It's my takeout order. I just stopped by to pick it up. I'm still working on the website, so I'll eat it at Fuzzy Friends," Brandon explained.

"You want to eat the pizza at Fuzzy Friends instead of HERE?! Well . . . okay. That sounds fine to me." I shrugged. "Actually, it would give us more privacy to talk. I'll let the waitress know."

"Thanks for the pizza and for the puppy drawings. They're AWESOME, Nikki! I planned to text you about them later today."

"I'm glad I could help out," I said. "Anyway, now that you're finally here, we REALLY need to talk. I tried to explain everything in my letter."

"Yeah, I got your letter," Brandon sighed. "I have to admit, after reading it I'm a little—no, I'm VERY confused."

"Just have a seat and we'll talk. I'll explain everything, including the photo drama, okay?"

"Sure. Although, to be honest, I think I owe YOU an apology," Brandon said shyly as he brushed his shaggy bangs out of his eyes. "You know, for the way I've been acting lately."

"Actually, I owe YOU an apology, Brandon."

"Listen, I agree we should talk. But I really need to go pay for this pizza with a gift card. I wouldn't want them to think I was trying to STEAL it!" Brandon joked.

"Yeah, my dad gave me some pizza gift cards too." I laughed. "I'm going to use one to pay for this meal."

"Okay, I'll be right back," Brandon said as he walked toward the checkout line.

That's when André returned.

"We're all set. The waitress is going to bring over some plates," he said.

"Good! So, um, thanks for the pastries and balloons. It's been nice talking to you, André."

Then, for some reason, he sat down at my table, picked up the menu, and started reading it. Then he kind of stared at me and smiled.

"So, I read your letter, Nicole. I realize we've only known each other for a week, but it feels like a year. I honestly never thought you'd feel the same way about ME that I feel about YOU!"

"OMG! André, YOU'RE having second thoughts about US spending the summer in Paris together TOO?! I'm SO relieved! This is really good news! I was hoping you'd understand!"

"Um, actually, I DON'T understand!" André mumbled. "I'm a little confused."

216

"Just like I said in my letter, if I change my mind, I'll let you know! Now, I think you should get to that party. I'd hate for you to miss out!"

"You keep talking about a party. WHAT party?!" André asked, getting a little annoyed.

"The one you said you were invited to. Don't you remember?"

That's when I heard someone clear their throat rather loudly.

It was Brandon!

He was back, and he did NOT look happy to see André sitting there. And André did NOT look very happy to see Brandon.

They both just stared at each other for what seemed like FOREVER.

Then the three of us had a really deep and meaningful conversation. . . .

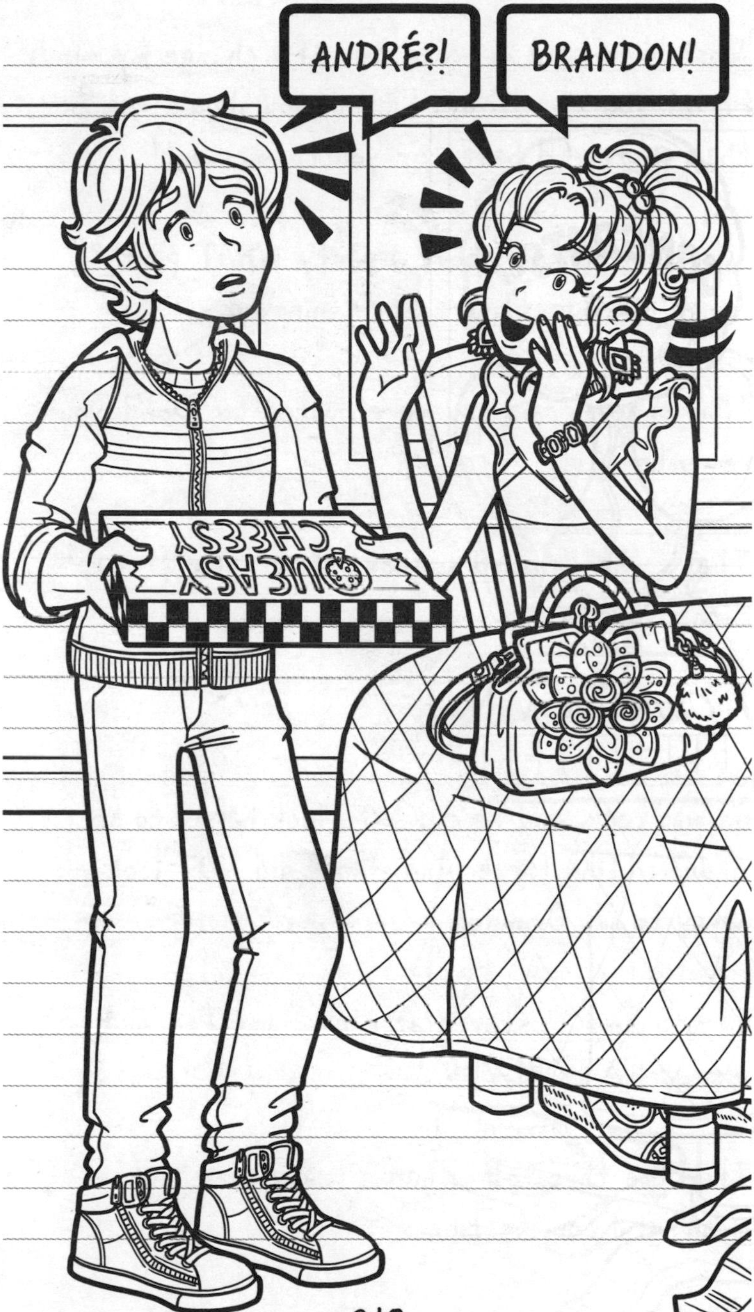
ANDRÉ?!
BRANDON!
CHEESY
QUEASY

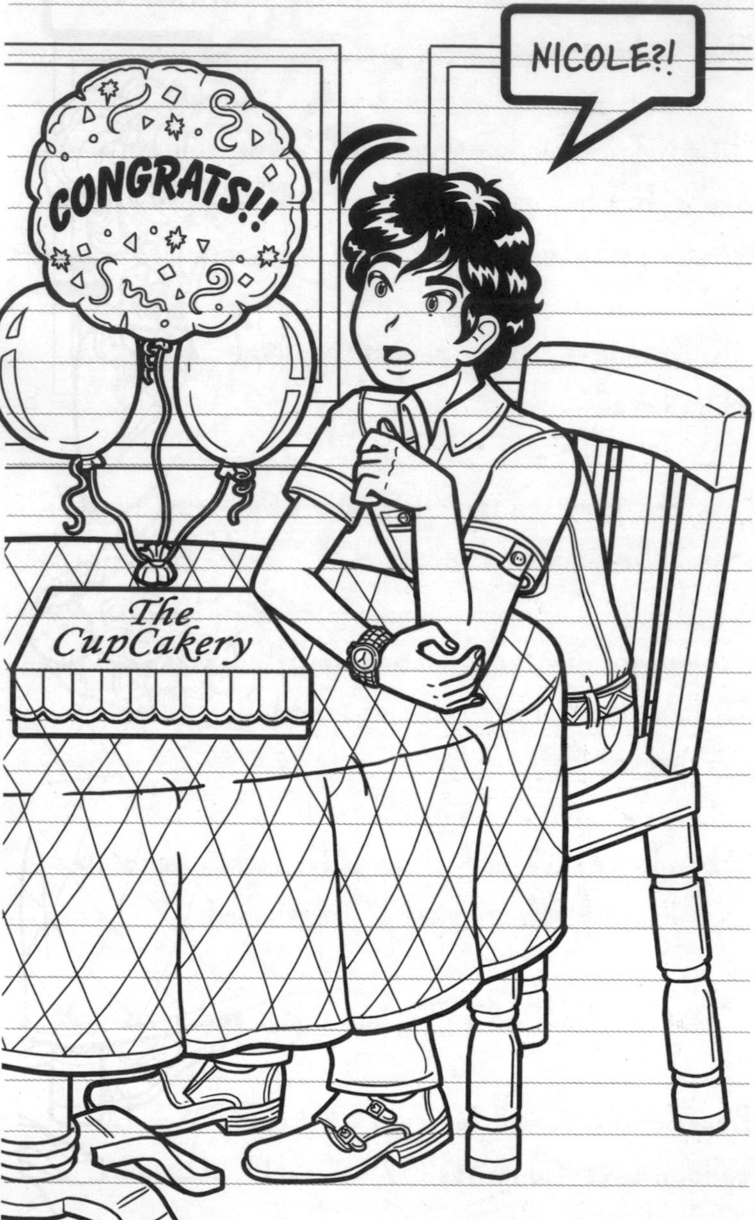
NICOLE?!
CONGRATS!!
The CupCakery

"So, Brandon," I said cheerfully. "Why don't you, um . . . have a seat?"

"I CAN'T!" Brandon grumbled. "André is in my SEAT! Again! It's becoming a really BAD habit, dude! What's up with that?!"

"Hi, Brandon!" André said drily. "What are YOU doing here?"

"No, the question is, WHAT are YOU doing in MY seat?" Brandon muttered.

I could not believe Brandon and André were acting SO immature. They were starting to get on my last nerve.

"Actually, André just stopped by to say hello. He's here for a birthday party," I explained.

"There. Is. No. PARTY!" André said under his breath.

Brandon narrowed his eyes at André. "So, the balloon says 'Congrats!!' What's the occasion?"

André folded his arms and grinned at Brandon.

"Nikki was awarded the trip to PARIS! It'll be fourteen days in mid-July, and I've volunteered to show her around the city! Didn't she tell you?!"

Brandon looked like he'd just gotten hit in the face with a dodgeball.

"Um . . . NO! She DIDN'T tell me! But what she DID tell ME was that she was going on the Bad Boyz tour the entire month of July, and I believed her. Although now I don't know WHAT to believe. Nikki, your letter is starting to make a lot more sense. . . ." Brandon trailed off as a wave of hurt washed over his face.

"Actually, André, I haven't had a chance to tell Brandon about the Paris trip yet!" I said.

"OOPS!" André shrugged. "SORRY!"

"Nikki, why didn't you tell me?" Brandon asked. "That's pretty important news! And it impacts ALL of our summer plans."

"Well, I tried to tell you, Chloe, and Zoey on Wednesday. And I tried to tell you again on Thursday, but you wouldn't even talk to me! That's why I wrote the letter," I explained.

"Okay, Nikki. I just have one question," Brandon said quietly as he stared at the floor. "Did you really mean what you said in that letter? I need to know that."

"Yes, Brandon, I meant every WORD of it. And I meant every WORD of the letter I gave to you, André. I would really appreciate it if you BOTH would let me make my OWN decisions. Just try to get along and stop acting like four-year-olds."

"You're right, Nikki," Brandon said solemnly. "I just want you to be HAPPY! And if it means Paris, then that's what I want for you. Listen, I'd better get going. This pizza is getting cold. So I'll . . . um . . . see you around. Maybe."

He turned and walked toward the door.

"Listen, Brandon. You don't have to leave. We still need to talk. At least I owe you an explanation. WAIT!" I said as I blinked back tears.

But Brandon just ignored me and kept walking.

He stopped at the door, glanced at me over his shoulder, and then opened it to leave.

At that moment it was quite obvious to me that our friendship, or whatever we had, was officially over ☹.

OMG! I can't believe it's after midnight. I'm mentally and physically EXHAUSTED just writing about all this stuff.

I'll think I'll finish this diary entry . . .

TOMORROW!

Right now I need to get some sleep!

☹!!

SUNDAY, JUNE 1—1:30 P.M.
IN MY BEDROOM

I still haven't quite recovered from all the drama at Queasy Cheesy. It was UNREAL!

Unfortunately, I won't have much time to write in my diary today because my mom is making me take Brianna to see *Princess Sugar Plum Saves Baby Unicorn Island: Part 9* ☹!

After that I plan to watch a marathon session of *My Very Rich and Trashy Life!* reruns, eat dinner, do my homework, and then go to bed.

Now, where did I leave off? . . . I was practically in tears at Queasy Cheesy as I watched Brandon walk away. He glanced sadly at me over his shoulder and then opened the door.

That's when my BFFs, CHLOE and ZOEY, came STORMING into the restaurant, YELLING like their HAIR was on FIRE!! . . .

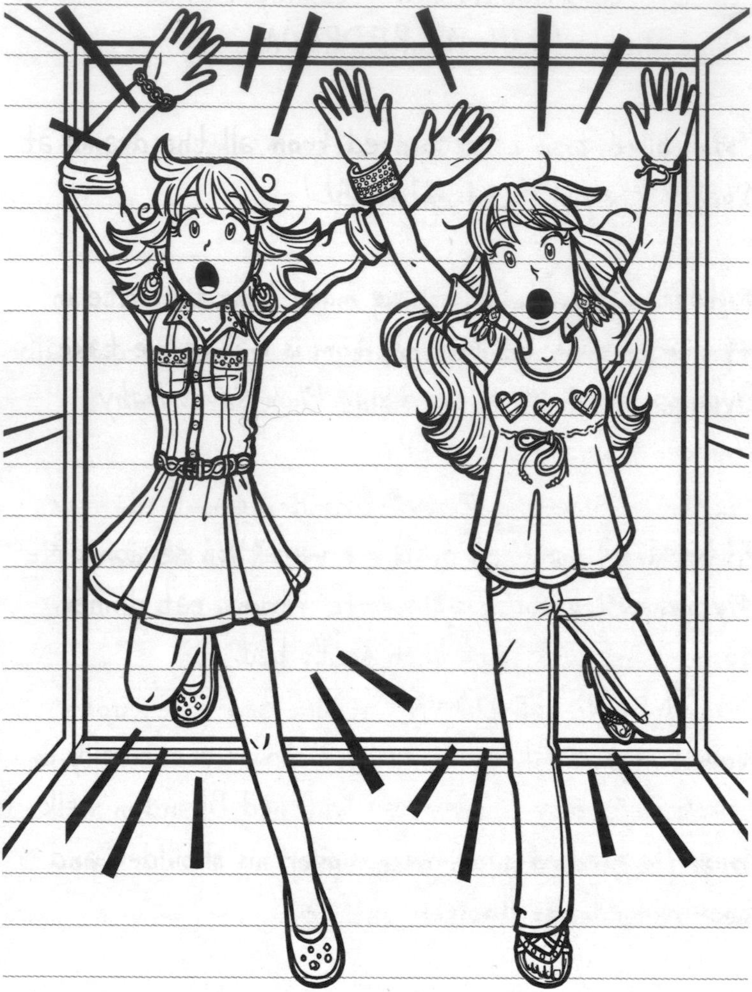

MY BFFS, CHLOE AND ZOEY,
ARRIVING AT QUEASY CHEESY

"OMG! Thank goodness we found you, Nikki!" Chloe shrieked, out of breath.

"We called your mom, and she told us you were here!" Zoey shouted excitedly.

WHAT in the world is going on? I wondered. Then they each grabbed Brandon by an arm and practically dragged him back to my table.

"Listen, Chloe and Zoey," Brandon grumbled, "the last thing I want to do is interrupt Nikki's date. So I was just leaving. . . ."

"BRANDON! SIT DOWN!!" Chloe and Zoey both yelled at him.

Brandon blinked in surprise, pulled up a chair from a nearby table, and quickly sat down.

"Listen, guys," André said, "I know you're really good friends and all. But Nicole personally invited ME here to discuss our summer plans. I think you need to respect our privacy."

That's when Chloe totally lost it. "Listen, Mr. Cutie Pants! You can talk to Nicole all you want. But stay away from our BFF, Nikki! I'm warning you! I know karate, kung fu, judo, tae kwon do, and at least five other dangerous words!" she growled.

"You tell him, girlfriend!" Zoey said. "And I'VE got . . . ! Wait, I know I put that thing in here somewhere," she said, digging around inside her purse.

Suddenly she whipped out her cell phone.

Just GREAT ☹! Chloe and Zoey barged in like a herd of wild buffalo and threatened my new friend, André, with violence!

JUST to take a few more cute SELFIES with him?!

I was SO disgusted!

Zoey tapped her phone a few times. "And I've got . . . THIS! An incriminating PHOTO!"

She shoved it right in André's face. "Can you explain THIS, André?!" Zoey shouted.

André stared at it and furrowed his brow.

"Um . . . it looks like a girl in pink pajamas with a mud mask on, dancing while singing into a hairbrush?" He shrugged.

"Oh, wait! That's me! Wrong photo!" She giggled nervously as she tapped her phone again.

Then she shoved her phone into André's face again. "Okay! Explain THIS!"

"Um . . . it's a little old lady with a party hat on, blowing out candles on a birthday cake?" he said.

"Oops! That's my grandma's seventy-fifth birthday party! Wrong photo again. This STUPID phone is so touch sensitive," she grumbled.

I just rolled my eyes. Brandon shook his head in disbelief. André looked a little bored.

"Okay, let's try this ONE LAST time! Explain . . . THIS!" Zoey snarled.

André glanced at the phone with a smirk on his face. But it quickly melted into concern. . . .

ZOEY, INTERROGATING ANDRÉ

Poor André, I thought. It looked like my BFFs had finally discovered those online photos of us.

Queasy Cheesy is known for its entertainment that features Queasy the Mouse and his rock band of animatronic animal pals. NOT my over-the-top middle school DRAMA!

But people were staring and eating popcorn ☹!

"Nikki, we're here to warn you that you're eating pizza with a DIRTY RAT!" Zoey said loudly.

Just at that moment, Queasy the Mouse was waddling by with a tray of pizza and heard her. He stopped in his tracks and sadly hung his head.

"Come on, Zoey! Queasy's a mouse, not a rat. And he's not THAT dirty," I argued. "Rodents have feelings too, you know."

"Actually, I wasn't talking about Queasy!" Zoey said. "Um . . . sorry about that!" She gave the costumed mouse a sheepish grin. "We GOOD?!"

Queasy gave her a nod and a thumbs—up and happily waddled away.

"I was talking about the two-faced WEASEL over there!" Zoey said, pointing.

I thought she was throwing shade at Willy the Weasel, who played guitar on the Queasy Cheesy stage. But she was pointing straight at André, who stared back with a worried look on his face.

"André?!" I uttered in shock. "Zoey, what are you talking about? You're making a BIG mistake."

Chloe tapped Zoey's shoulder. "I'll take it from here. I got this!" she said gruffly, like the bad cop. Uh-oh, I thought. Chloe is my BFF and all, but sometimes that girl can be so . . . EXTRA!

"So, Chloe and Zoey, would you like one? They're delish!" André said nervously as he offered them his box of French pastries.

"Dude, the ONLY reason we're here is to . . .

TAKE. YOU. DOWN!" Chloe said, wagging her finger in his face. "Nobody messes with our BFF! Even if they've got delicious, melt-in-your-mouth chocolate pastries that are still warm and smell heavenly!"

She snatched the box of pastries from André and shoved one into her mouth. . . .

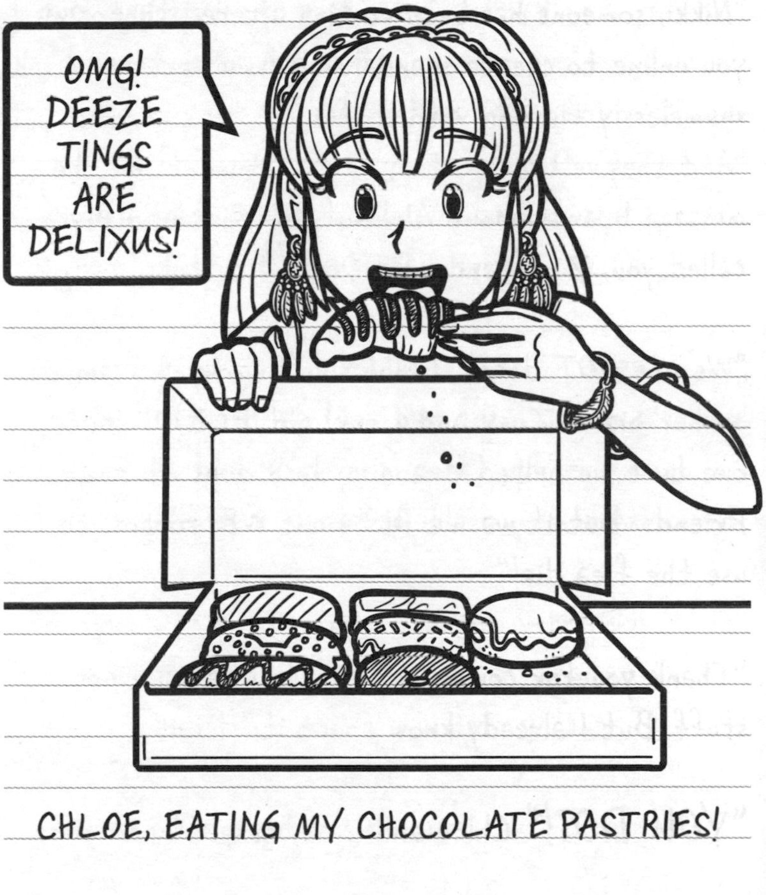
OMG! DEEZE TINGS ARE DELIXUS!

CHLOE, EATING MY CHOCOLATE PASTRIES!

"I'm confiscating these for . . . um . . . evidence!
I need to taste test each one for safety reasons!"
Chloe muttered with her mouth full.

"Chloe, CHILLAX!" I shouted. "Leave André alone!
And PLEASE tell me what's going on!!"

"Nikki, someone has been posting altered photos of
you online to create scandalous gossip about you
shamelessly flirting with André," Zoey explained.
"And they've been posting nasty comments on the
message boards about ALL of us. They actually
called you, Zoey, and me DOGS!"

"We are NOT dogs!" Chloe said angrily, her hands
on her hips. "Zoey and I only got FLEAS that
one time we helped Brandon wash dogs at Fuzzy
Friends. But it wasn't HIS fault WE forgot to
use the flea dip!"

"Thank you for coming here to tell me all this
stuff. But I already know about it," I said.

"YOU DO?!" Chloe and Zoey gasped in surprise.

"Yeah! Brandon does too. And you just told André.
I think SelfieChic is Tiffany and MacKenzie is
LuvMyLipGloss. MacKenzie pretty much admitted
to me she posted the pics. But I'm sure she's going
to LIE like a rug if we report her to Principal
Winston for cyberbullying. We're going to need
more PROOF!"

"Well, here's another piece of the puzzle for you!"
Zoey said as she showed Brandon and me that photo
on her phone.

I'd assumed it was one of the photos of André and
me online, but it WASN'T!

OMG! I could NOT believe my eyes! It was . . .
SHOCKING!

The four of us just GLARED at André like he
was something nasty Daisy had left behind the
couch.

"Listen, that photo is NOT what it seems. Nicole,

234

you've got to b-believe me! I c-can explain!" André
stammered.

"Okay, André. You have exactly ONE minute,"
I said, trying to remain calm. "Start EXPLAINING!"

Maybe there WAS a perfectly innocent explanation
for what we saw in that photo ☺! But from the
looks of it, probably NOT ☹!

UH-OH! My mom just called me.

I have to stop writing now.

Time to go on an EXCITING trip to Baby Unicorn
Island for yet another CAPTIVATING adventure
with Princess Sugar Plum and my bratty little
sister.

WHY was I NOT born an only child?!

!!

MONDAY, JUNE 2—NOON
IN THE JANITOR'S CLOSET

I thought I knew André pretty well. He seemed like a really nice guy, but I guess I was wrong.

I had been happy to hang out with him because he said he'd just started attending North Hampton Hills and didn't have any friends.

He had also confessed that he hated being the "new kid" and was really worried about fitting in.

I felt the EXACT same way when I first came to Westchester Country Day Middle School.

OMG! It was **HORRIBLE!** The first few weeks of school, I wandered the halls like a **ZOMBIE!**

No one ever talked to me and I sat alone at lunch every single day. MacKenzie always went out of her way to make my life MISERABLE!

So Chloe's cell phone pic kind of blew my mind! . . .

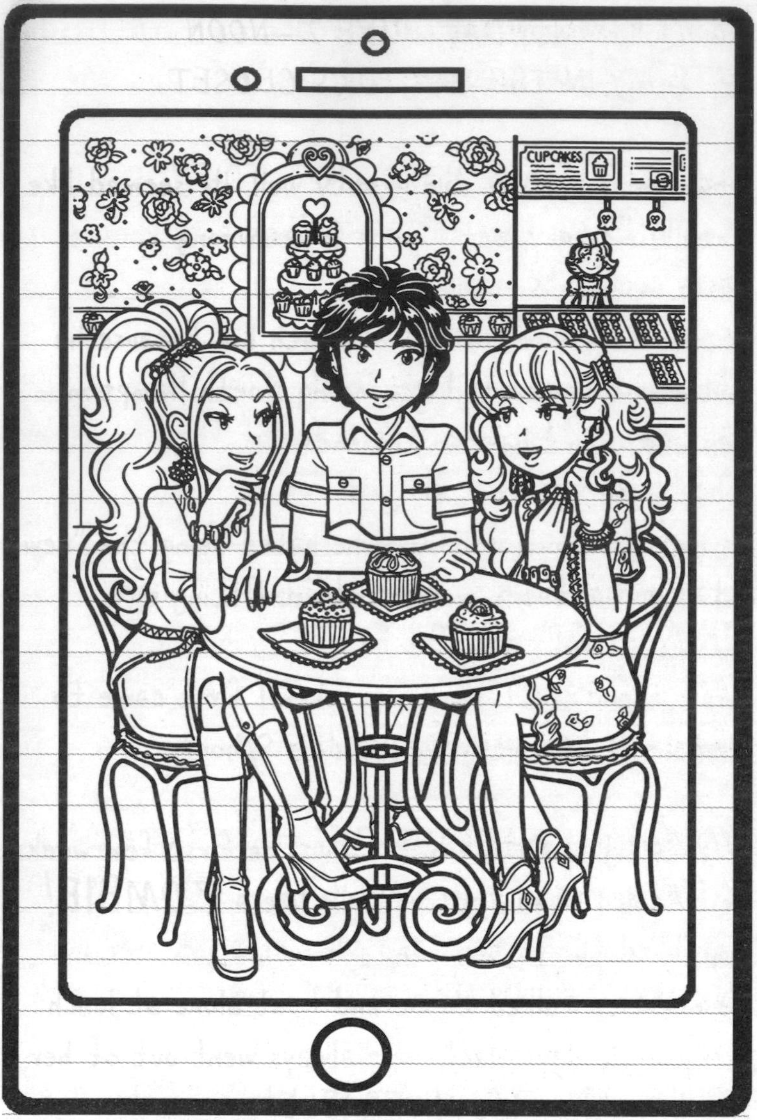
CUPCAKES

ANDRÉ AT THE CUPCAKERY WITH MACKENZIE AND TIFFANY?!

I don't know why, but BOTH MacKenzie and Tiffany HATE MY GUTS ☹!!

And now it appears that André is FRIENDS with them AND has been HELPING them post photos and nasty comments online.

Chloe and Zoey had been at the CupCakery earlier that day and had seen the three of them together. They'd snapped that pic just for me.

I felt numb. I was so hurt and upset, I wanted to CRY!! I really thought he was my friend.

André was talking, but I wasn't really listening.

". . . so I just sat down at their table for a minute just to see what they were up to and say hi. Then I grabbed the pastries and came straight over here. And that's the truth, Nicole!"

The four of us just stared at André silently. Then Chloe cleared her throat. "André, would you like to know what we're thinking right now?"

He smiled weakly and looked hopeful. "Sure, Chloe. I'd love to hear what you have to say."

"ANDRÉ, THAT'S THE MOST RIDICULOUS STORY WE'VE EVER HEARD AND A COMPLETE PACK OF LIES, YOU PATHETIC CYBERBULLY!" she yelled.

"Listen, I'm sorry you guys don't believe me. But that's NOT going to stop me from doing the right thing!" André said, getting up to leave. "And, Nicole, I'll always . . ." He looked at Brandon and stopped midsentence.

I don't know why, but I suddenly felt REALLY confused. What if André was telling the truth?

We watched as André walked to the door.

He glanced sadly at me over his shoulder and then opened the door.

That's when MacKenzie and Tiffany came barreling through the door, yelling at the top of their lungs like they had lost their minds. . . .

"ANDRÉ! YOU THIEF!! YOU ARE SO BUSTED!" MacKenzie yelled.

"GIVE ME BACK MY PHONE! NOW!" Tiffany screamed. "I KNOW YOU TOOK IT!"

They each grabbed him by an arm and practically dragged him back to our table. My friends and I just stared at them, speechless. WHAT was going on?!

The biggest question was, when had MacKenzie and Tiffany become members of the I HATE ANDRÉ CLUB? They were ALL at the CupCakery just an hour ago, CANOODLING like BFFs. Something was very FISHY!

"You know what, Tiffany? I DON'T believe you for one second!" I said. "YOU stole Mr. Winter's lesson plan book and then told him that I did it, remember? And NOW you're saying André stole your phone. You may not be a pathological LIAR, but I bet you're really close!"

"Tiffany, I totally agree with Nikki," Brandon said.

"I HATE to admit it, but I don't think André stole your phone! He may be a cold, deceitful, backstabbing cyberbully, but I don't think he's a dirty, rotten, sleazy THIEF."

Chloe and Zoey nodded in agreement. . . .

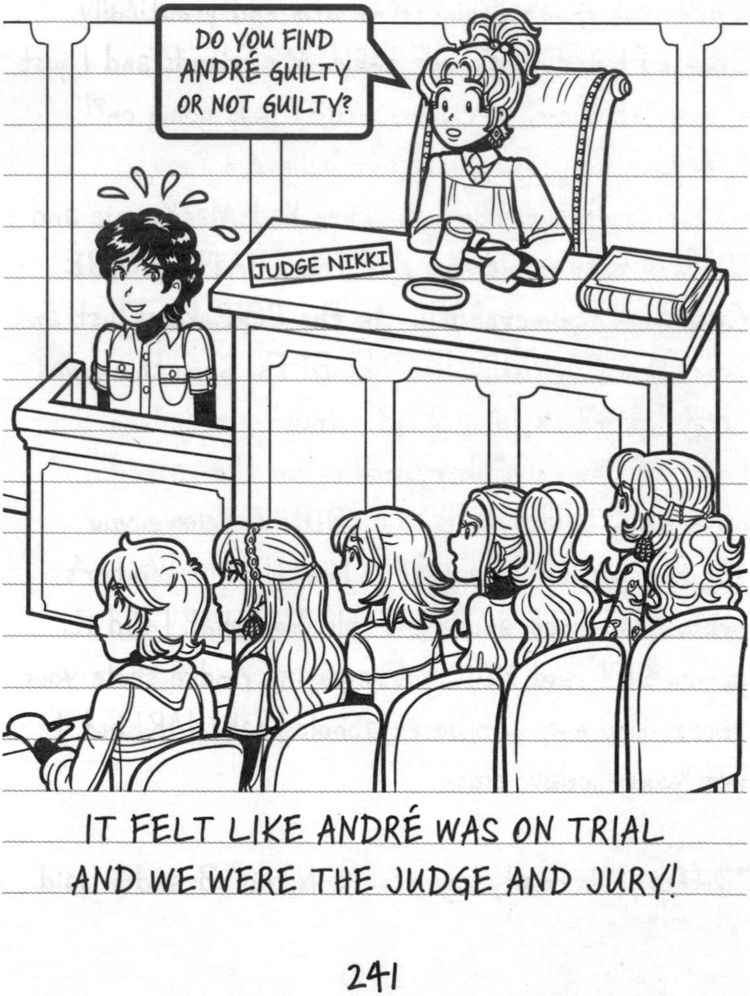
DO YOU FIND ANDRÉ GUILTY OR NOT GUILTY?
JUDGE NIKKI

IT FELT LIKE ANDRÉ WAS ON TRIAL AND WE WERE THE JUDGE AND JURY!

But what happened next ALMOST made my head EXPLODE!

"Actually . . . I AM a dirty, rotten, sleazy THIEF!" André confessed, like it was NOT a big deal.

THEN HE ACTUALLY PULLED TIFFANY'S CELL PHONE OUT OF HIS BACK POCKET!

Everyone gasped! I could not believe my eyes!

"See, Nikki?! I told you André was shady!" Chloe exclaimed. "Someone call the POLICE! Quick!"

"Just let me explain, okay?" André pleaded. "While I was at the CupCakery picking up the pastries, I overheard Tiffany and MacKenzie talking about the photos they'd posted online. I saw them posting nasty comments on some website using Tiffany's phone. So I just kind of borrowed it so I'd have proof of what they were doing. I'll give it back to her later today."

"Dude, isn't that illegal?" Brandon said.

"How do we know you didn't STEAL those pastries, too?!" Chloe shrieked. "OMG! I've been eating STOLEN property! I'm going to JAIL!"

"You're NOT going to get away with taking MY phone, André!" Tiffany yelled. "You mess with me and you're going to be in BIG trouble! Give it back right now! Or I'm . . . I'm telling MOM!"

"No you're not, Tiffany!" André shot back. "Because . . . I'M TELLING MOM!! Sorry, but you're BUSTED! For cyberbullying people again! I have all the proof I need right here. Mom will probably ground you for half the summer and make you do community service at the senior citizens center. Just like last time!"

"André, don't you DARE tell Mom! PLEEEASE!" Tiffany whined. "I HATE volunteering at the senior citizens center. I'd rather EAT five tubes of denture cream and DROWN myself in a bucket of PRUNE JUICE than go back there!"

"Hold up! Hold up! Hold up!" Zoey interrupted.

"Tiffany, Imma let you finish!" she said, like that famous rapper. "But . . . ANDRÉ IS YOUR BROTHER?!!"

My head was SPINNING!

"I'm her STEPBROTHER!" André answered. "My mother is married to Tiffany's father."

That's when my head actually EXPLODED!! KA-BOOM!!

"Who needs pizza?! This is an all-you-can-eat DRAMA buffet!" Zoey said, shaking her head.

"Tiffany, what you and MacKenzie did was just . . . CRUEL!" I was SO angry, I could, um . . . SPIT!

"OMG! Are you seriously trying to shame me for cyberbullying right now?" Tiffany scoffed. "My cell phone has been STOLEN and my summer has been RUINED! That makes ME the real VICTIM here! And HOW am I going to get my hourly SELFIE fix with no cell phone, Nikki?!!"

"Sorry, girl, but I'm not sorry!" I shot back.

"Tiffany, I'm shocked! How could you be so mean to Nikki?! Dorks have feelings too, you know!" MacKenzie said, creeping toward the door. "I'd love to stay longer, but I need to go home and wash my hair and get my beauty sleep! Toodles!"

"Oh, no you don't!" Tiffany grabbed MacKenzie's arm. "Shampoo isn't going to fix your raggedy split ends. You need a car wash! Besides, how could you bail on your BFF like this?!"

"Well, no shade, Tiff! But I don't really know you like that!" MacKenzie said coldly. "Besides, Jessica is my real BFF, not you. So whatever."

"Fine! Who needs a BFF like you, anyway?" Tiffany spat. "And, girlfriend, you don't need beauty sleep to fix that face! You need to HIBERNATE! Until next SPRING! And before you leave, why don't you tell everyone how you snuck into Nikki's backpack and SWITCHED Brandon's and André's letters?! If I'm going DOWN, you're coming WITH me!"

MacKenzie just glared at her. "Tiffany, all that gossip about you being a ruthless backstabber is true! My cell phone BATTERY lasts LONGER than your FRIENDSHIPS!"

MACKENZIE AND TIFFANY
HAVE A MEAN GIRL SPAT!

Then MacKenzie turned to me. "Nikki, you were right about Tiffany. She IS a bigger liar than I am! I feel SO sorry for her. I'd hug her, but I don't want to get DUMB on my arms! I'd much rather be friends with you."

It was quite obvious that MacKenzie was just trying to weasel her way out of the mess she and Tiffany had made.

André had been oddly quiet.

"Um . . . Tiffany, what did you mean about the letters being switched? So I got the one meant for Brandon?"

"That's right, Romeo. Don't tell me you thought Nikki was really into you!" Tiffany laughed cruelly. "She didn't invite YOU to Queasy Cheesy, she invited Brandon! MacKenzie has the IQ of an orange crayon, but she played you both like a video game. You lovesick losers will fall for anything!"

Both André and Brandon looked shocked.

So **THAT** was why they'd both been acting so strange ever since they'd gotten my letters.

I felt really bad for them both.

"Listen, guys, I'm really sorry about the letters. You didn't deserve that, and I apologize."

"No need to apologize, Nicole," André replied. "I'm sorry if I was a bit, um . . . . overbearing. I was just a little confused, I guess."

"Same here," Brandon said. "If anything, WE both owe YOU an apology, Nikki!"

"Guys, you know what I WANT more than an apology? For you two to get along and STOP fighting over SEATS!" I teased.

"Listen, André, I was wrong about you," Brandon said. "You're not a cyberbully or a thief. You're really a cool DUDE! For a French guy, anyway."

"Likewise, my friend." André smiled back. "For you

to have figured all that out means you're pretty smart. For an American dude, anyway."

Then they gave each other a high five. I just rolled my eyes at them. At least they were now acting like six-year-olds instead of four-year-olds.

"AH . . . ACHOO!" Chloe fake sneezed. "Nikki, you don't want the rest of these pastries, do you? I just accidentally sneezed on them! Sorry!"

"I love happy endings!" Zoey gushed. "Who's up for a group hug?!"

Zoey, André, Chloe, Brandon, and I all huddled into a big group hug while Tiffany and MacKenzie brooded behind us.

"This whole thing was YOUR stupid idea!" Tiffany complained. "And now my summer is RUINED!"

"No, it was YOUR stupid idea!" MacKenzie grumbled. "You're the one who's obsessed with posting SELFIES on social media!"

"Well, get used to it, girlfriend! We'll BOTH be taking A LOT of selfies together this summer when we're FORCED to volunteer at the senior citizens center!" Tiffany shot back.

Tiffany and MacKenzie totally DESERVE each other.

In spite of all their mean girl drama, I managed to survive my Not-So-Secret Crush Catastrophe!

OMG! I've been in here writing for so long, I'm late for bio!

I gotta go!!

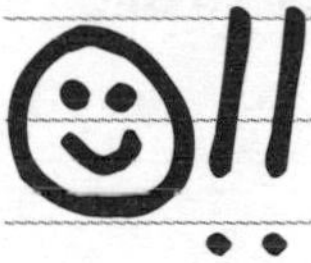

TUESDAY, JUNE 3—5:30 P.M.
IN MY BEDROOM

Today was the last day of school!

SQUEEEE ☺!!

Which means that my SUMMER VACATION has officially started!

Brandon came over to give Daisy another doggie obedience lesson. I think they're really helping, and I've noticed a drastic improvement in her behavior lately.

Today was a socialization session for Daisy so she could learn to get along with other dogs.

Brandon brought over three dogs from Fuzzy Friends to hang out with her.

But, unfortunately, Brandon and I got a little distracted. I think WE probably did MORE SOCIALIZING than the DOGS did. . . .

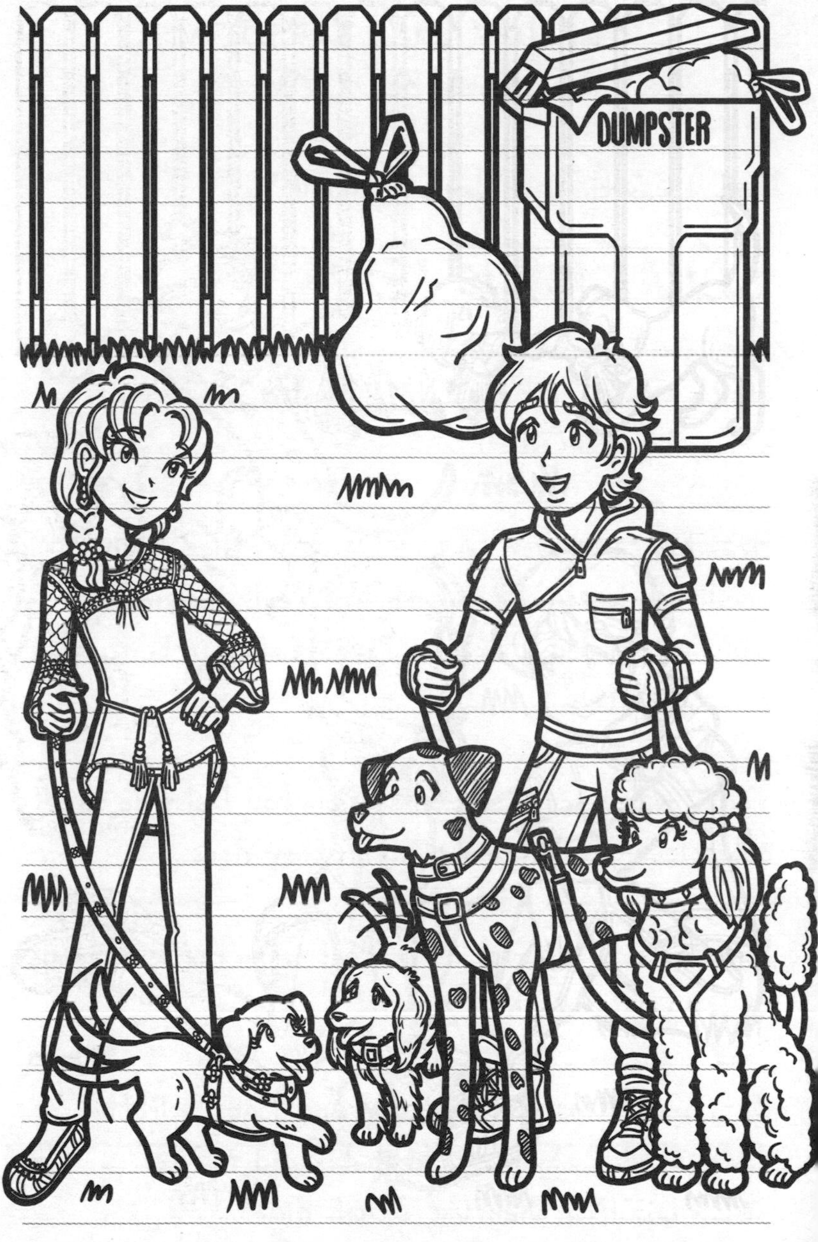
DUMPSTER

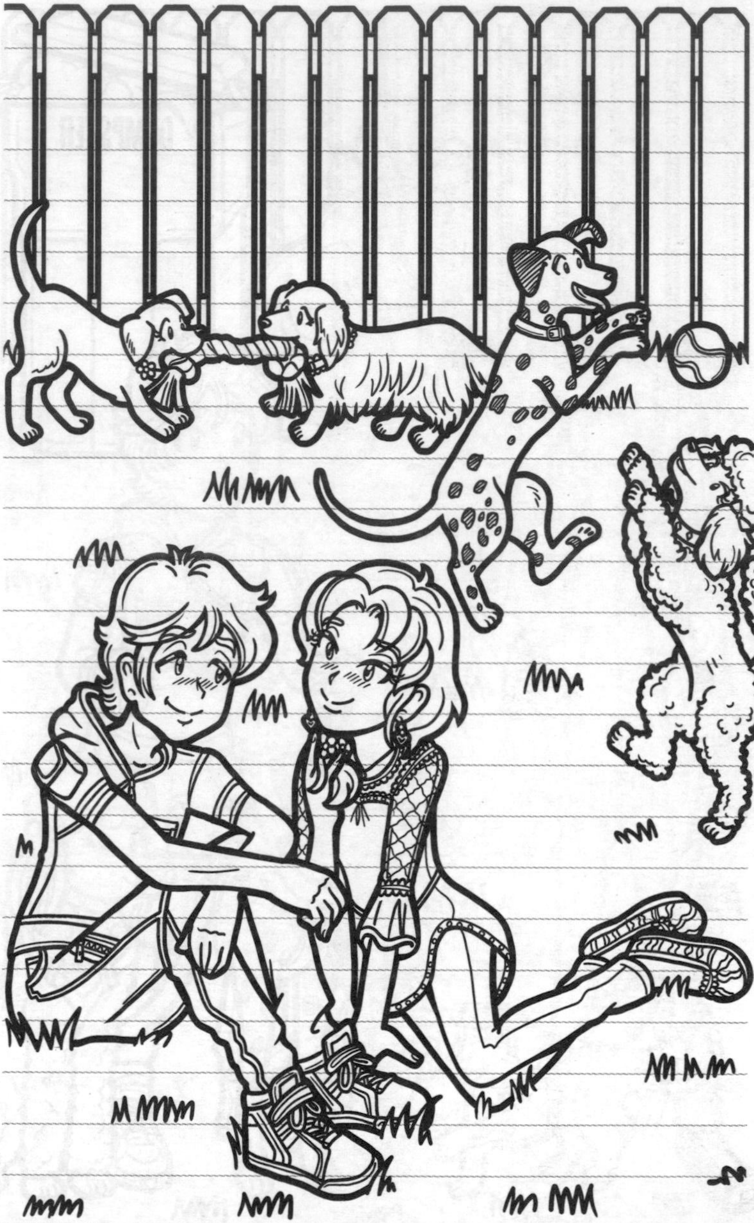

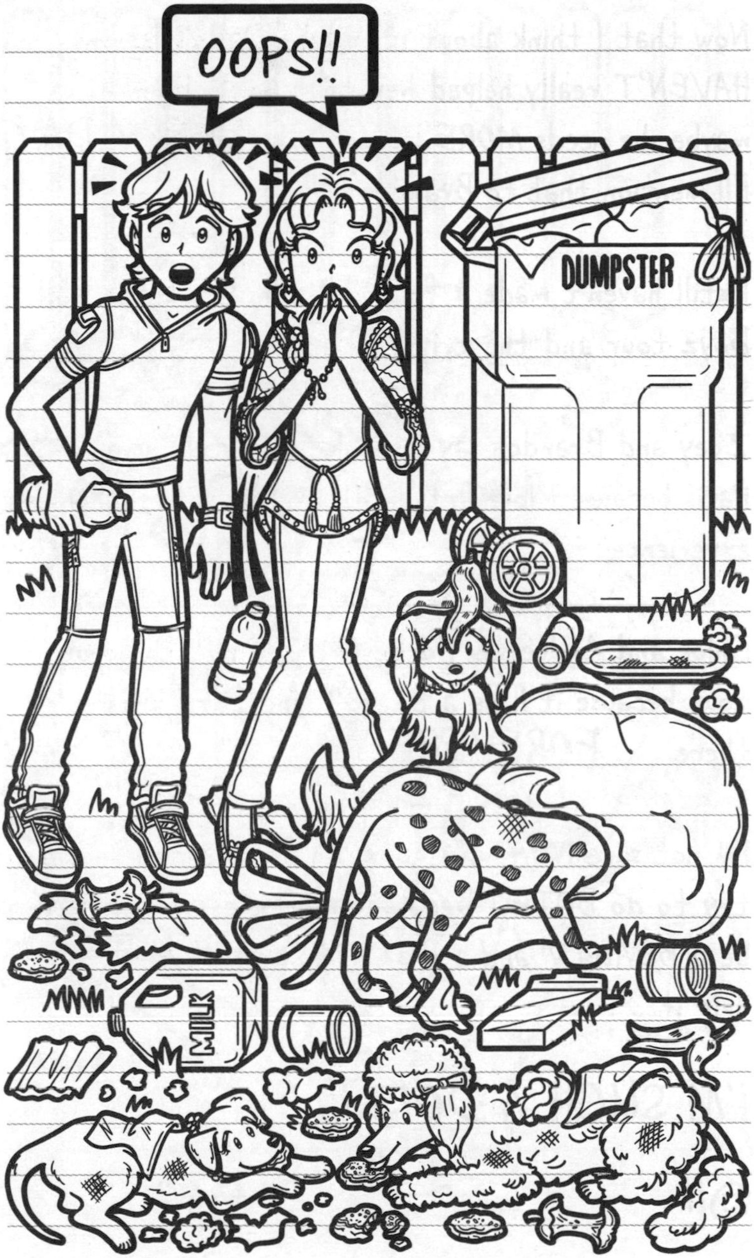
OOPS!!
DUMPSTER
MILK

Now that I think about it, maybe Daisy's lessons HAVEN'T really helped her that much. Hmm . . . maybe she needs MORE lessons. Like EVERY DAY. I'll mention that to Brandon ☺!!

I still haven't made a final decision about the Bad Boyz tour and the trip to Paris.

Zoey and Brandon say I should definitely go to Paris because I love art and it will be a life-changing experience!

Chloe and André say I'd be CRAZY not to go on tour because it'll be a BLAST and Paris will be there . . . FOREVER!

I'm not sure WHAT I'm going to do. Maybe I should try to do BOTH?! Because sometimes you gotta be a BEAUTY and a BEAST! Sorry! I can't help it. . . .

I'M SUCH A DORK!!

☺!!

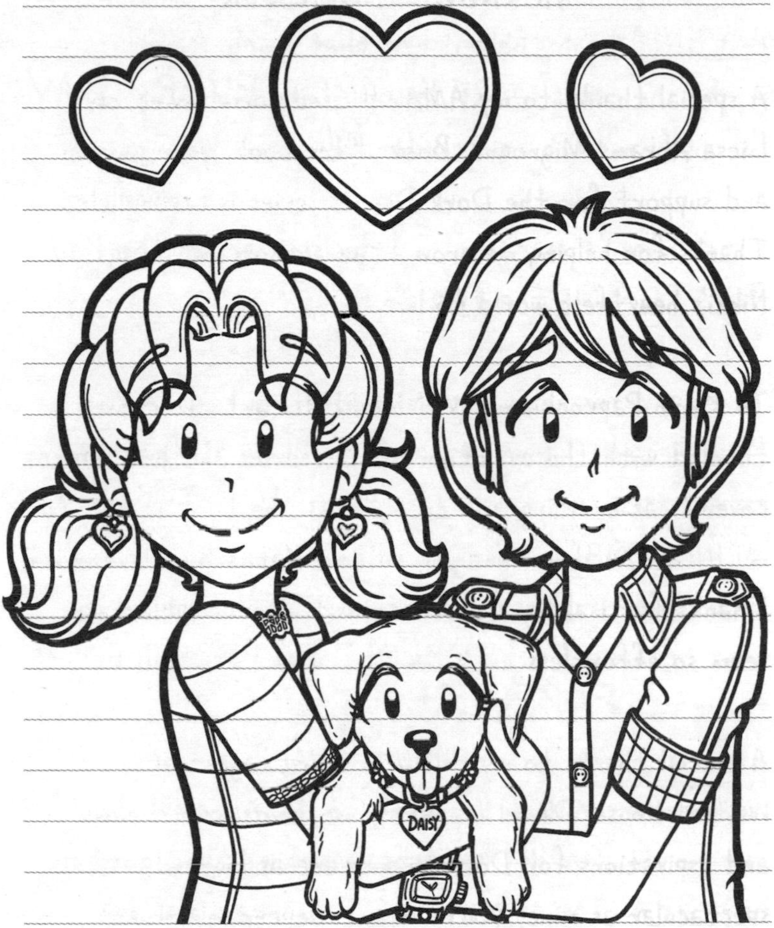
DAISY

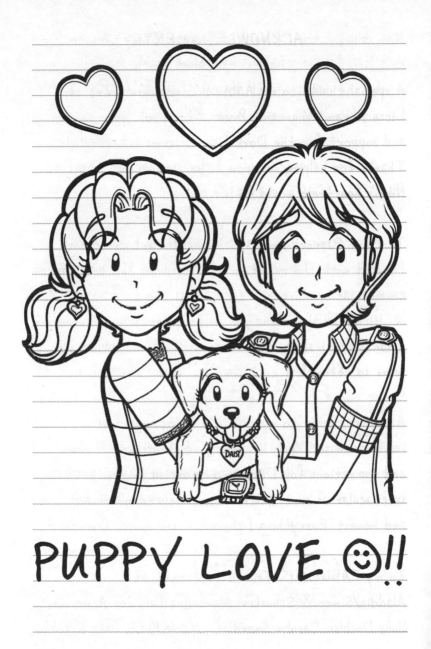

PUPPY LOVE ☺!!

ACKNOWLEDGMENTS

A special thanks to my AMAZING editorial director, Liesa Abrams Mignogna. Book after book, your passion and support for the Dork Diaries series is unparalleled. Thanks for helping me grow as an author and bring Nikki's heartfelt world to life.

To Karin Paprocki, my WONDERFUL art director. I'm thrilled with the evolution of our series and how each cover is as exciting and creative as the book itself. To my INCREDIBLE managing editor, Katherine Devendorf. Thanks for making a difficult and inconceivable task seem so effortless.

A special thanks to my PHENOMENAL agent at Writers House, Daniel Lazar. I love that your dreams and aspirations for Dork Diaries are as big and spectacular as mine! You're smart, dependable, funny, and honest. Everything I cherish in our great friendship.

To my FABULOUS Team Dork staff at Aladdin/Simon & Schuster: Mara Anastas, Jon Anderson, Julie Doebler, Carolyn Swerdloff, Nicole Russo, Jenn Rothkin,

Ian Reilly, Christina Solazzo, Rebecca Vitkus, Chelsea Morgan, Lauren Forte, Crystal Velasquez, Michelle Leo, Anthony Parisi, Christina Pecorale, Gary Urda, and the entire sales force. Thanks for all of your hard work and dedication. You are truly irreplaceable.

A special thanks to my Writers House family, Torie Doherty-Munro and foreign rights agents Cecilia de la Campa and James Munro, for your world-class support. And to Deena, Zoé, Marie, and Joy, thanks for your collaboration.

To my gifted and creative illustrator, Nikki, and to my super-talented and witty coauthor, Erin: I consider myself very lucky to be able to work side by side with my dorky daughters, who inspired this book series. And to Kim, Don, Doris, and my entire family! Thanks for your love and for championing all things Dork Diaries.

Always remember to let your inner DORK shine through!

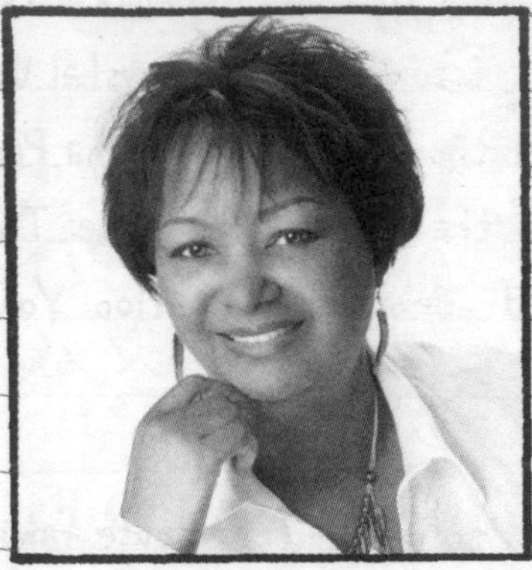
PHOTOGRAPH © BY SUNA LEE

Rachel Renée Russell is the #1 *New York Times* bestselling author of the blockbuster book series Dork Diaries and the bestselling new series The Misadventures of Max Crumbly.

There are more than thirty-six million copies of her books in print worldwide, and they have been translated into thirty-seven languages.

She enjoys working with her two daughters, Erin and Nikki, who help write and illustrate her books.

Rachel's message is "Always let your inner dork shine through!"

Do you love

DORK
diaries

and reading all about Nikki's
not-so-fabulous life??

Then don't miss out on the
BRAND NEW series from
Rachel Renée Russell!
featuring new dork on the block,

MAX CRUMBLY!

Rachel Renée Russell
the misadventures of MAX CRUMBLY
Locker Hero
Rachel Renée Russell
the misadventures of MAX CRUMBLY
Middle School Mayhem
from the creator of DORK diaries
SIMON & SCHUSTER

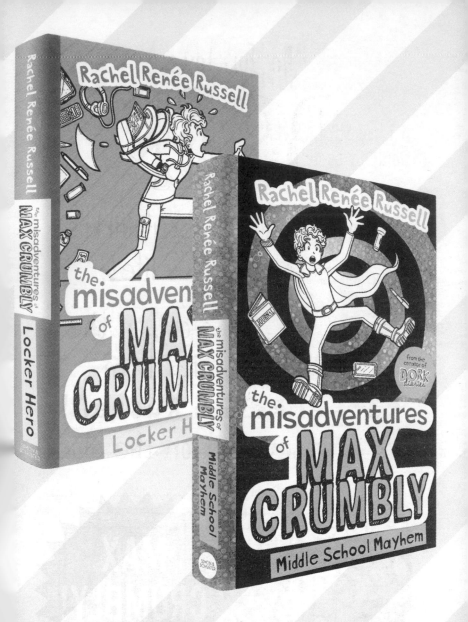

"If you like Tom Gates,
Diary of A Wimpy Kid and, of course,
Dork Diaries you'll love this!" *The Sun*

1. MY SECRET LIFE AS A SUPER~~HERO~~ ZERO

If I had SUPERPOWERS, life in middle school wouldn't be quite so CRUDDY.

Hey, I'd NEVER miss the stupid bus again, because I'd just FLY to school!...

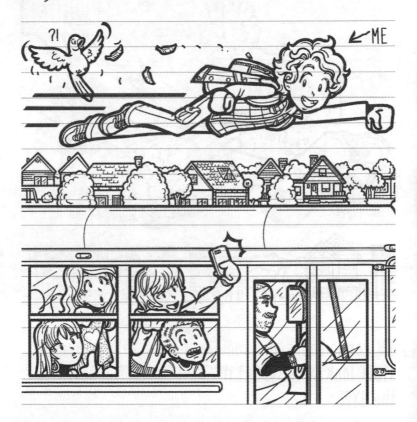

AWESOME, right? That would pretty much make ME the COOLEST Kid at my school!

But I'll let you in on a secret. Getting bombed by an angry bird is NOT cool. It's just . . . NASTY!!

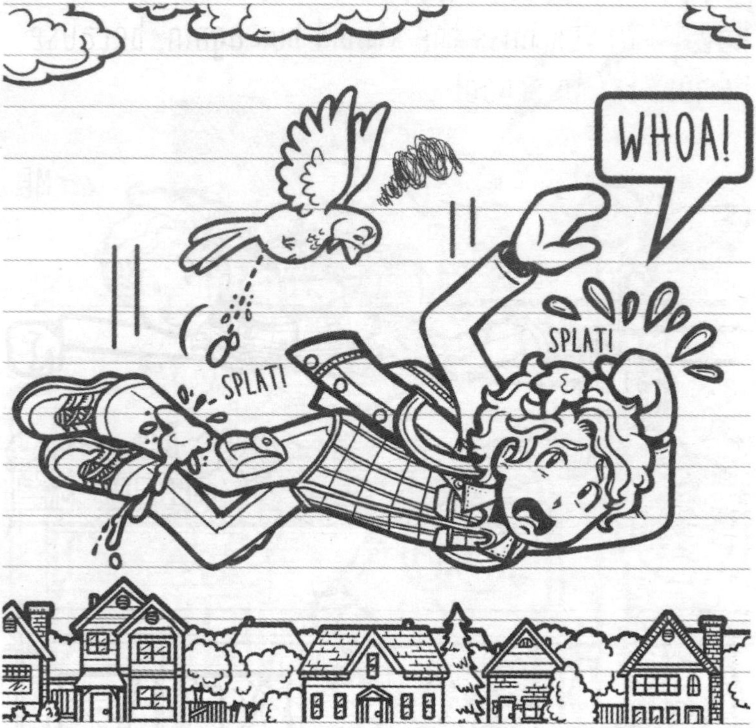
WHOA!
SPLAT!
SPLAT!

TV, comic books, and movies make all this superhero stuff look SO easy. But it ISN'T! So don't believe the HYPE.

You CAN'T get superpowers by hanging out in a laboratory, mixing up colorful, glowing liquids that you simply DRINK. . . .

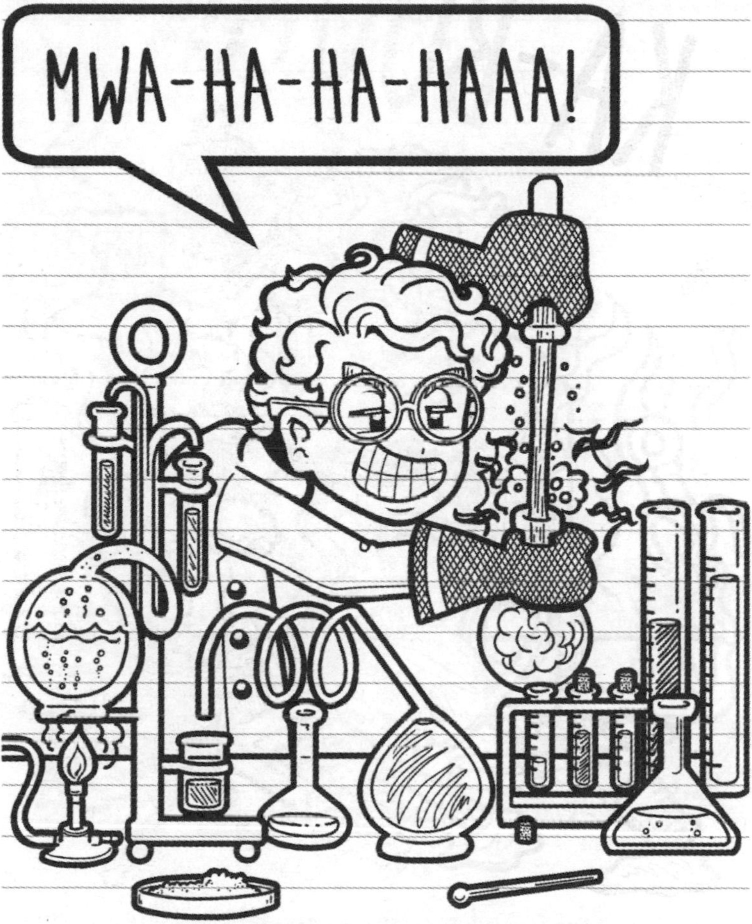
MWA-HA-HA-HAAA!

ME, MIXING UP A YUMMY
SUPERPOWER SMOOTHIE

HOW do I Know it doesn't work? . . .

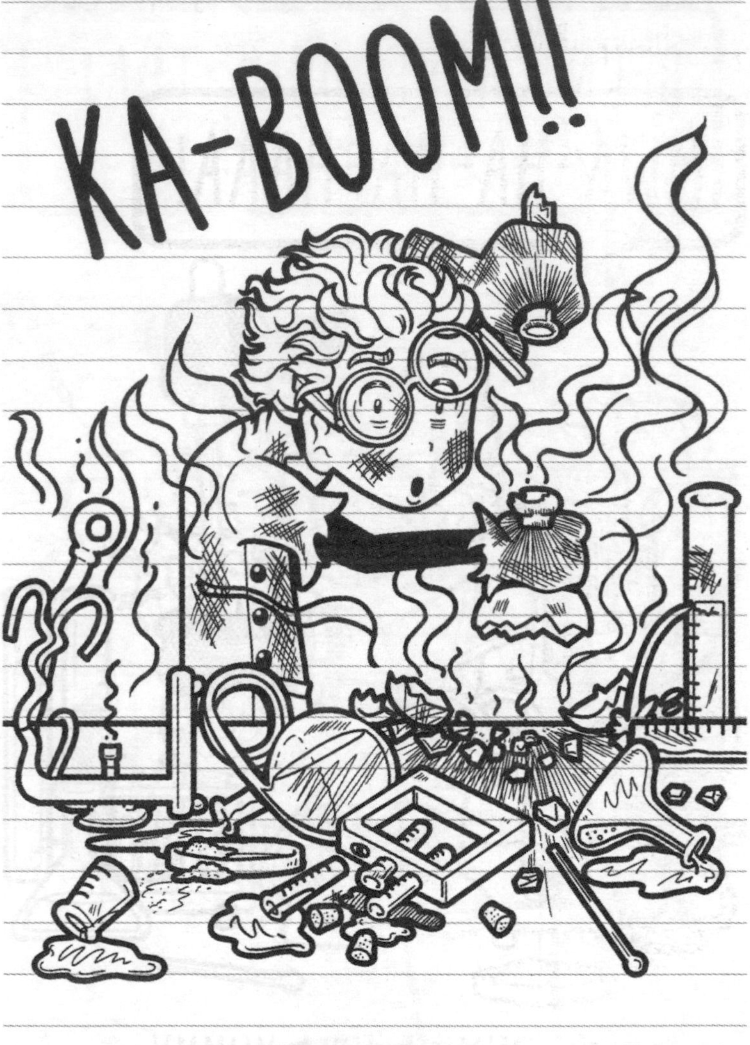
KA-BOOM!!

"OOPS!"

Let me put it this way. . . .

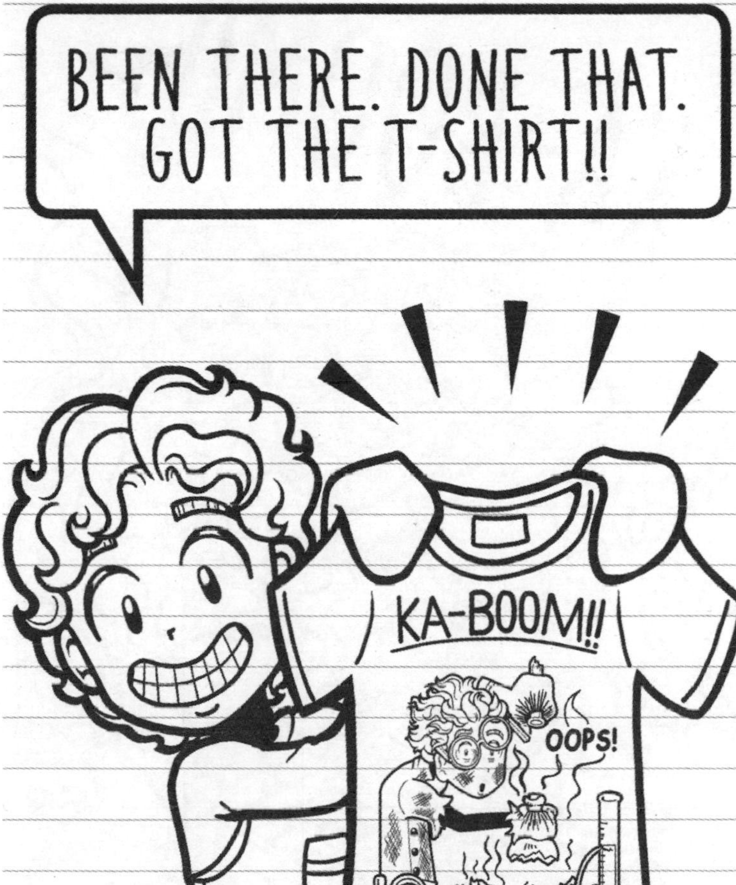
BEEN THERE. DONE THAT. GOT THE T-SHIRT!!
KA-BOOM!!
OOPS!